She looked up a e
bird had left s(-
dered if any part o. ι,
pondering what the bass would prefer. She tucked the bird under the hydrangeas. After filling her cup with more worms, she ran to the river bank to join her brother.

A few days later, Molene awoke to the sound of raindrops pelting her window. She lay still, her little sister's feet pressed against her back, and studied the way the raindrops swerved around the smudge left by the bird. She waited until she heard Mamzy in the kitchen, putting on a kettle of coffee, and then she slunk out through her window.

Her feet sank into the earth, and the scent was one of her favorites. That after-rain smell. But something else tried to sneak in there. Something rotten. Something dead. Molene felt around under the hydrangeas and found the little bird. Mamzy could name every bird in Posey County just by listening to its song, or seeing it flit by. Molene wished she'd paid attention. It seemed like the thing might have been a chickadee, but she couldn't be sure. It really wasn't a bird anymore. Just a carcass. Some of its feathers were still intact, but one side looked like an open wound. Little dark organs hid behind delicate white bones. Maggots squirmed inside, and even as Molene held the thing, flies buzzed and tried to alight upon it. She began scooping moist earth to make a shallow grave with one hand. She'd really only meant to bury it. But as she moved to place the chickadee in its shallow grave, her fingers touched the bones.

Copyright © 2019 by Marianne Halbert
ISBN 978-1-950565-52-8
All rights reserved. No part of this book may be used or reproduced in any manner whatsoever without written permission except in the case of brief quotations embodied in critical articles and reviews
For information address Crossroad Press at 141 Brayden Dr., Hertford, NC 27944
A Macabre Ink Production -Macabre Ink is an imprint of Crossroad Press.
www.crossroadpress.com

First edition

COLD COMFORTS

BY MARIANNE HALBERT

Story Publication History

"When Betsy Whispers" (originally published by The Four Horsemen LLC in *Anthology: Year One*, 2015)
"Papa's Wrench and the Wind Chime" (originally published by Mocha Memoirs Press in *The Grotesquerie*, 2014)
"Like Riding a Bicycle" (originally published by Evil Jester Press in *Help! Wanted: Tales of On-the-Job Terror*, 2011)
"Luxor Decanted" (originally published by Great Old Ones Publishing in *Canopic Jars: Tales of Mummies and Mummification*, 2014)
"Housing the Hollygobs" (originally published by Necon eBooks in *Now I Lay Me Down to Sleep*, 2017)
"The Fourth Movement" (original for *Cold Comforts*)
"'Neath Fallow Ground" (originally published by Pill Hill Press in *Back to the Middle of Nowhere: More Horror in Rural America*, 2010)
"Adverse Possession" (originally published by Grinning Skull Press in *From Beyond the Grave: A Collection of 19 Ghostly Tales*, 2013)
"The Fire Tower" (originally published by The Horror Society in *The Horror Society Presents: Abandoned Places*, 2015)
"Conjuring the Corpse Candles" (originally published by Static Movement in *Fall Shudders*, 2011)
"Hey, Karen" (original for *Cold Comforts*)
"A Used Infinity" (originally published by Stygian Publications in *Necrotic Tissue: The Horror Writers' Magazine*, April 2010)
"A Bone to Pick" (original for *Cold Comforts*)

Dedication

To Steve, Olivia and Chloe. My perpetual comforts.

Contents

When Betsy Whispers	1
Papa's Wrench and the Wind Chime	10
Like Riding a Bicycle	24
Luxor Decanted	32
Housing the Hollygobs	46
The Fourth Movement	54
'Neath Fallow Ground	65
Adverse Possession	80
The Fire Tower	91
Conjuring the Corpse Candles	101
Hey, Karen	115
A Used Infinity	123
A Bone to Pick	137

WHEN BETSY WHISPERS

She was always Betsy.
She learned the art of whispering from her mother. The darkness opened, revealing a blinding blue sky above. An unsettling fear of the unknown made her want to scream. Then the rest of the world fell silent, a slight breeze began to blow, and her mother's tender branches cradled her, gently rocking her back and forth. Her mother's leaves shifted and stirred, whispering sweet nothings to Betsy. Occasionally her mother would weep for the siblings lost to the frost, but then she would resume her melancholy lullaby, sung for Betsy alone. One night, before the hour of sunrise, the wind became an angry gust, and ripped Betsy from her mother's grasp. The umbilicus severed, she felt herself falling, helpless, carried away through the pelting rain.

The earth felt cold and unwelcoming. In the distance, Betsy heard her mother's frantic cries as her branches whipped back and forth in the torrent, the sound of her boughs cracking as she desperately reached for her lost child through the storm. But the effort was fruitless.

Betsy was alone.

Streaks of jagged light split the sky, and thunder exploded overhead. Frightened and forsaken, missing the pulse of life she'd been connected to, Betsy sought protection. Each time she tried to move, she was pounded back into the ground by the downpour. Exhausted by the effort, she relented and lay still in her new bed until just before the dawn. Upon waking, aching for devotion, she split open, and sent forth a sweet tendril. If that kind of love could no longer find her, she would find it.

Digging, searching, Betsy's misery wouldn't end until she was someone's sole object of affection again. At first nothing. Hours went by. Weary, she dozed in a pre-dawn haze. Then there it was. Something nudged her awake. A night crawler. It slid, stretching and constricting, rubbing against her. Basking in euphoria at the long-awaited contact, Betsy didn't realize the creature was mindlessly moving away until it was almost too late. With a toddler's greed, the only thought she could formulate was, *Mine*. And then it was in her grasp. A part of her knew she was gripping too tightly, but the thing wanted to slither away from her. Desperate for its love, she felt its struggle. Its flailing movements only made her grasp harder. She felt its life force fleeing it, and flowing into her. She grew stronger. As the first rays of day found her, she reached upwards.

Her roots continued to feed on the subterranean, but over the coming years, Betsy grew unsatisfied with bugs and slugs. As she branched out, she witnessed squirrels scampering and birds flitting among her cousins. *She* wanted to attract these lively creatures. She morphed from stout to lithe, and grew fine branches, perfect and strong. And she remembered her mother's gift. The way she could make any being on Earth feel as though they were the most loved. *The only one.* Fortunately for her, she was a fast learner. She sprouted leaves, waited for the slightest breeze, and began to rustle.

Betsy whispered.

Welcoming, soothing, she lulled small creatures up her trunk. Onto her boughs. Noses twitched. Whiskers quivered. She craved the feel of a critter nestling inside her. The warmth, the heaving. The heartbeat. But inevitably, her appetite overcame her and she took the life, absorbing it, letting it nourish her. Like any addict, she was never satisfied. She craved more.

One day men on horses drew near. They were like no other prey she'd stalked before. They were watchful. They had a pecking order. The men looked around for the most comfortable spot to take a rest. And to plot.

The air was still, the other trees lifeless, yet Betsy rustled her leaves, showing off her best side. *Here*, she sighed softly. They had almost passed her by when one of the men pulled on the reins of his mare, and crooked his head. His eyes studied the other trees, then landed on her. Timid, she spoke up again. *Here. Yes. I'm the one you're looking for.*

Without a word, the man's commanding eyes brought the others back. They dismounted, the leader arching his back. The pack settled in near Betsy's trunk, and drank in her shade. One of them leered at her lowest branch. It wasn't long before he began to drool.

"That's the one," he said.

The leader followed his gaze. He stood, brushing dirt from his pants. He walked around her, eyeing her from every angle. Admiration, and a glimmer of excitement shone in his eyes. He tested her strength, then nodded his approval. Betsy experienced a surge of carnal longing when they mounted their horses and departed.

They returned hours later, and she shivered with yearning, remembering their touch. One man tossed a rope over her thickest branch. The others helped to tighten it. It bit into her bark. Betsy's roots quivered with anticipation. One end of the rope went around the neck of a man on a cart directly beneath her. He struggled, and she inhaled, drinking in his essence. The cart moved, unloading him, and she felt the weight of him under her. The spasmic movement as he flailed. *Such a life force!* He extended one hand up, as though if he could just grip her, the suffering would stop. His fingertips brushed her flesh, sending a tingle down her trunk, all the way to her roots. Minutes passed. He weakened, then quieted, going limp. Betsy shuddered, her leaves rustling, shuddered once more, and felt at peace.

She heard one of the men. "Yep, that's the one." And that's how Betsy became the hanging tree.

Over the years, more men came. Each time she heard their approach it was like the rap of a suitor's knock at her door. When they stopped and she knew it was going to be another hanging, it was like a lover's brusque hand brushing the sleeve off her shoulder. She came to look upon the men on horses as servants, bringing her nourishment. When she felt the rope cinch around her, she held her breath in anticipation of that sweet joining of her life and another's. She hungered for the rush of vitality those lovers provided, however brief the engagement. The coupling was always bittersweet, as Betsy realized early on, they were never going to be anything more than a one-time encounter. Then one day, the men on horses didn't bring a rope or a suitor. They brought an axe.

The first blow was the most excruciating. The men chopped her apart. Raw, she wanted to cry out, but they severed her branches, abandoning her beautiful leaves in the dust. Crying thick, sappy tears, Betsy was defenseless as they sawed her into beams and planks. Men hauled her away and erected her at the far end of town, almost out of reach of the gentry. Steps, a platform, braces and uprights. They pounded on her and drilled into her until she took on her new form. Bereft of her dignity and her voice, Betsy silently cursed their very existence.

But then a man with a gold star pinned to his chest climbed her steps. He stood on her platform, and caressed one of her uprights slowly, so slowly. He clapped another man on the back. "Fine work, gentlemen. Most gorgeous scaffold I've seen yet." He paused before walking away and rubbed her once more. Whispering just to her. "Gorgeous."

Betsy soon discovered she no longer required leaves in order to whisper. Even though she stood on the outskirts of town, there were now always men about. They were drawn to her. She could convince them to touch her, to stroke her. To bring her sacrifices. Now when her lovers came, she had an audience. The crowds' eyes were ravenous with lust. Betsy groaned as the door dropped, and the horde cried out in a frenzied fervor.

Over the years, there were fewer and fewer hangings. Betsy hungered. Then the men came again with saws. She felt their hands on her, tugging at her. They took her away. Under cover of darkness, they escorted her beyond a sharp-wired fence secreting acres of nothing but a few large brick buildings. Carelessly, they tossed her onto the floor.

"Use the braces and uprights for the back and legs of the chair. Make the seat and arms from the platform." The man barking the order commented on how appropriate it was that the chair should be forged from the gallows.

Two men in identical blue denim went to work on her.

One with dark eyes examined each plank, each post. As hours turned to days, Betsy admired his thick dark hair, the cut of his jawline, the way his muscles flexed when he lifted her into his arms. She'd never had the luxury of studying a man in such proximity for extended periods of time. And all the while, he studied her too, letting his fingers stroke the grain of her wood. She'd never felt so exposed before. So intimate.

"Hank, back to your cell. It's time for lights out," a voice called from the hallway. "It's not like that heap of wood is going anywhere." Hank lingered. He put his fingertips to his lips and then gingerly pressed them to her, leaving Betsy with her first kiss. The sound of his receding footsteps was a like a dagger.

Betsy came to covet the moments when Hank was near. The other man treated her like she was nothing special. Just a piece of furniture. But Hank...Hank approached her delicately. She whispered about how he was the one. *The only one.* He was so careful with every inch of her. She relished the pain in his eyes when he saw how the other man had drilled into her. So protective. He became so critical of the other man's mishandling of her that eventually Hank became the only one allowed to touch her. Alone at last, he slid his palms over the curve of her arms, and used his tools to shape them until they were perfectly smooth and uniform. He selected only the best black leather to cover her seat, the finest brass buttons for her chastity belt, securing the gentle swell of leather into place. He insisted on fastening them himself.

"Lucky you," a guard said to Hank. "Out of here in a few weeks. Don't worry. We'll christen her good." Betsy didn't like the man's lewd chuckle, and was relieved when he left the room. Hank's eyes looked pained and shimmery. *Don't leave me,* she whispered. He carved notches out of her footrest. *Be with me.* He hesitated, then carefully sat down in her lap. *Stay with me.* He exhaled, lay his head back against her, closing his eyes, and eased his ankles into the notches. A perfect fit. *Yes...we're a perfect fit.*

The days moved quickly. Hank massaged oil onto Betsy's surface. He began to mumble. "I got privileges now, darlin'.

Could be out in the yard." He rubbed her harder. "Or taking visits with my sister. But none of that," he said, choking up. He swiped the back of his hand across his cheek, staining himself with her perfume. His touch was softer when he reached for her again. "None of that seems to matter now." His voice sounded haunted as he went on, nearly hoarse. "Tomorrow doesn't matter now." He collapsed to his knees, his head dropping into her lap, and as she held him, he wept. Then he was gone.

An electrician came one morning, and put his hands on her. Groping, he bound cords to her neck and ankles. Betsy ached for Hank. She had learned to whisper without wind. Without leaves or even branches. Heartsick, in her mind she reached for him. *Find a way,* she pleaded. *Find a way back to me,* she implored.

After weeks of despair, Betsy heard the men talking about Hank's return. How there was no motive for the murder. But he'd done it, plain as day. In front of a dozen witnesses. He insisted his lawyers offer no defense. He declined a last meal. All he wanted was Betsy...and to die in her arms. Betsy didn't disappoint.

He hadn't seen her in months. It wasn't allowed. It was bad luck for the groom to see the virgin bride before the wedding. Shackled, he stepped in the room, and hesitated. She knew he was just allowing himself that extra moment to inhale her beauty.

When Hank sat down, they were a perfect fit as they'd always been. Like honeymooners, spooning. He relaxed into her, his muscled back pressing against her chest. Straps bound his wrists to hers, but he didn't struggle. His fingers flexed, then gripped her arms for comfort. Someone dipped a sponge in water, and placed it over his scalp, the water dripping as Betsy grew moist.

Betsy didn't care about the onlookers this time. All she knew, all she cared about, was Hank was with her again. In her arms at last. Suddenly a jolt went through her, an explosion of energy, and Hank shuddered. His muscles tensed and he went rigid, thrusting into her. Betsy felt alive like never before. Hank's life, his love, penetrated her. Ravenous, Betsy's only thought was *mine mine mine.* Again. She wanted him again and again.

But Hank lay still. Too still.

Men unbound them and took Hank away. His essence was already fading within her now, and she knew he wouldn't return. She wanted to take it back. To bring him back. To feel his hands on her again. Someone turned off the lights and the door closed. Betsy no longer smelled of woody perfume. She smelled of burnt death. Confined to solitude, Betsy was alone once more.

She agonized over her loss, and found her only solace in the suffering of others. Hank had taught her the first sound of foreplay. The clanking echoes of feet approaching the adjacent room. Sometimes the voice was silent. Others were wailing, or begging. Betsy had come to enjoy the begging. The carnal scent of a last supper. Some came to her resignedly, others were cajoled or even dragged. But none were like Hank. None sought her out. Not for years.

Then one night, during a violent storm, a man was brought to the adjacent room. Betsy whispered to him through the wall. He waved away dinner and moved closer to the wall. Betsy shared with him her most intimate thoughts. Promised him a higher and more profound ecstasy than he'd ever known. He waved away the priest.

When the man stood in the doorway, he gazed upon her. One of the guards was new and young, and it pleased Betsy when he flinched at a clap of thunder. He had a milky, lazy eye that seemed to roam, searching for the source of the boom, but the other eye, blue as the sky that had welcomed her into the world, was trained on Betsy. The young guard mentioned the storm outside, how it was a real gale.

Come to me.

The prisoner lowered himself onto Betsy. The guard shifted his head, ever so slightly, confused. He pulled on his earlobe. "Hey, did any of you hear—"

A second crack of thunder pounded overhead, and the lights cut out. Betsy latched on to her partner and didn't let go.

When the lights came back on, the older guards pronounced the man dead. But with no electricity during the power outage, they didn't understand how he could have been electrocuted.

The boy with the lazy eye looked at Betsy like she might bite him, and silently backed out of the room.

Then there came the dry spell. For a time, Betsy feared her fleeting moments of arousal were over when, according to the rumor, men's laws made her forbidden. She felt obsolete. She whispered to the men in black robes, and eventually the court saw the error of their ways. For twenty more years she felt purpose. The boy with the lazy eye grew into a man as he reluctantly brought her more victims. Betsy brought terror to some. But to those susceptible to her whisper, those who waived their appeals and last-minute stays from the governor, she brought the ultimate joy.

The guard, her guard, walked into her room one day, unannounced. There had been no clanking of chains. No scent of a last supper. His blue eye focused on her. "You've seen your last victim. Lethal injection is taking your place." He didn't smile. He didn't seem victorious. Just cautiously relieved. "Store her in the catacombs," he said. "She no longer gets to see the light of day." Two young men dragged her away.

Betsy was relegated to a dank dungeon. She spent those dark years settling for the spiders and rats that crawled across her lap. Splitting and cracked now, she recalled how beautiful she had once been. She fantasized about the many men she'd known. She replayed stolen moments with Hank. But mostly, she grew nostalgic for those early days in her mother's arms. *If only*...then a long-rusted door creaked open. Hands were on her once more.

It had been years since Betsy had breathed in the open air. The sun's rays warmed her as she was moved across the yard. She heard the shushing of leaves trying not to gossip as she passed beneath them. She yearned for those mornings under the open blue sky. The chirping of birds carrying on their own conversations. Then a shadow passed over her and that door closed.

A lazy eye searched for her from a wrinkled face, and a piercing blue eye under a snow-white brow found her.

"I want her placed behind soundproof glass," he said. The man, hunched over with age, began to scuffle away toward the door.

"You mean shatterproof, right?" asked a youthful freckle-faced man. "So no one who visits the museum will damage it?"

Betsy perked up at the sight of the young man's dimples, and his fiery hair. She wondered, for the first time in years, if she could still—

"I mean soundproof," the old man growled as he turned on her. He stared her down with his one good eye, standing as tall as he could manage with his brittle back. "That glass isn't there to protect her from the public."

Betsy smiled. And she whispered to her old friend. *No indeed. It's to protect them from me.*

PAPA'S WRENCH
AND THE WIND CHIME

The patch of fog on the window, expanding and fading with each breath, was the only proof that I was still breathing as the school bus turned the corner. The driver slowed, and the brakes made a squeaking, squealing sound. It reminded me of the mice my brother used to feed to his snake. Of that sound they made before the fangs released a blessed silence. Most of the kids, including me, were sitting two to a seat. We were still a block away and had just passed the Dead End sign when I heard the wind chime. Dainty at first. It always sounded dainty at first. Then clanging as the breeze picked up. I knew what hung from that oak tree. We all did. And we knew what was making that sound.

Every time we drew near that house, I thought of this old album my mom put on the turntable at Halloween. Sound effects like creaking floors, screeching cats, and a thunderstorm played as a woman with an overly dramatic, yet convincing voice described a "dilapidated" house. It was only mid-September now, but I heard that woman's voice in my head. I looked at the Monstrum place, with its drooping gutters, missing shingles, and peeling paint. I mouthed the word *dilapidated*, and the patch of fog on my window grew again.

The bus rolled to stop. The Monstrum kids stood motionless, waiting, behind a broken porch banister. They all had a certain look about them. Lanky, with long straight hair that had never seen a barber's shop or a beautician's blade. Some said they all wore black eye shadow on their upper lids, but I was among those convinced the lids themselves were a smoky black. The older ones wore gloves all the time, and spoke through practically closed lips. I watched the horde of them descend those warped front porch steps. In one motion, like a flock of birds, they moved across their overgrown front lawn. Dandelion seeds scattered on the wind, and a few of the Monstrum girls blew kisses after them. A shiver ran through me at the thought of those wishes being granted. Gunther, the oldest boy in the group, led the V formation.

My gaze moved from the horde to that tree. I studied the weapons dangling from its branches. I'd looked at those items, watched their numbers grow, even gazed through a set of binoculars as I huddled down in the seat a few years ago. All the usual items were there today. A rusted hacksaw. Hunting knives that had been scarred by whatever it was they'd stabbed. Tire irons, one of them bent in perpetuity at an awkward angle. Two long guns with jagged, splintered grooves in the wood, a bayonet, and a tomahawk. Hundreds more. I looked back at the clan. The older ones should have broken off from the group and headed toward their van by now. But they hadn't.

Marla leaned in closer to me, gripping my arm.

"Ginny, what are they doing?" She was practically hyperventilating and her breath smelled like sour milk. Her voice was verging on shrill. "They can't all be riding the bus today. They can't…there's too many of them."

I looked at the rusted blue VW bus they usually drove to school. Something was wrong. It was lopsided. I let out a slow breath, fogging the window again.

"Flat tire."

The weapon wind chime clanged again, and Gunther smirked, revealing just a hint of yellow teeth. One of his younger brothers, a raven-haired boy I didn't recognize, broke from the formation and ran back into the house. The rest of the group had almost reached the bus. I could hear whimpers and gasps from my schoolmates. The few kids sitting on their own looked around, eyes frantic. They scattered and found safety sitting with friends. Marla scootched even closer to me. I glanced around and saw three empty seats. Three empty seats for the entire Monstrum clan. It wouldn't be enough.

Gunther stepped up and into the school bus. His brown eyes darted around, his brown hair dangling over his shoulders. He stood aside, letting some of his siblings settle in to the three empty seats. But more were coming. They began to sit with other kids. Twin sisters, with matching scarlet gloves, and their white-blond hair elaborately braided together, took the seat in front of me. Once they were all settled, Gunther sauntered toward us. He sat down next to Marla. She let out a yelp and climbed over the back of the seat. I was all alone as he sat beside me.

I squeezed as close to the window as I could. I didn't want to look at those weapons anymore. I didn't want to know how they'd gotten there, how they'd gotten chipped or bent, or what had happened to their original owners. As the bus driver began to make his three-point turn, I stared down at the plastic pink ring on my finger. But a flash from the Monstrum yard caught my eye.

One of the twins mumbled, "Eugene's not going to make it." She craned her neck to look out the window, and because her sister was tethered to her via the braid they shared, she craned her neck also.

I watched the boy race for the bus, his long black hair flying. He looked so pale. So frail. Kindergarten? First grade at the most. The bus had completed the turn and was trundling down the road, but the boy was fast. As we were about to make the turn, the Dead End sign behind us, he pounded twice on the door. The driver cranked the door release, and Eugene Monstrum clambered aboard.

He didn't have any books or a backpack, so I couldn't imagine what he'd forgotten that had made him run back to his house. The bus accelerated, but he remained steady on his feet. His eyes met mine and I froze. *Not here. Not two of them. Please not two of them.*

Eugene stepped forward. His small chest heaved twice. Whether he was recovering from his sprint for the bus, or preparing to challenge his brother, I can't say. But he looked Gunther in the eye. "This. Seat's. Taken." Eugene took two more

deep breaths, and this time it made me think of how animals puff themselves up in anticipation of a challenge.
Gunther didn't say anything for a minute. He didn't seem angry. If anything, he seemed puzzled, and a bit amused. I could see that smirk of his in the driver's rearview mirror. Eugene had to reach up to put one hand on the back of the seat. The look on his face, his posture, seemed to be saying "Are you going to make me repeat myself?"
Gunther shook his head and stood up. He swept one gloved hand in my direction. "She's all yours, little man."

I should have known by the smirk on Carl's face that this was coming. To his credit, he let Papa finish saying grace. He even waited until the plate of pork chops had gone around the table before he started in.
"So," Carl said, "I heard the bus ride to school this morning was interesting."
I felt my face flush. I kicked my brother under the table, but that only elicited a giggle from him. Papa was tucking his napkin into his collar when he turned to me. His brows were as fiery red as his hair, and he raised them as he casually said, "Oh?"
I gritted my teeth, seething at my older brother.
"Apparently the Monstrum kids rode the bus this morning," Carl said.
Mama shook her head. "The Monstrum kids always ride the bus. Those of us on the school board tried to put a stop to it years ago."
Then Carl blurted it out. "*All* of them."
I watched Mama's face. She held the gravy boat in one trembling hand. A blob of gravy plopped onto the white tablecloth and she didn't even notice. I could see the wheels turning in her head. She knew Carl had gotten a ride to school with his friend Scott. She turned to me in slow motion, almost like she was afraid to look at me. Afraid of what she'd see.
"*You* were there?" She tried to set the gravy boat down but missed the table and it shattered on the floor. "Did any of them get near you?" She was already rising out of her chair. "Did any

of them *touch* you?" Her voice sounded thick, like she was trying to keep herself from throwing up.

Before I understood what was happening, she raced upstairs. The sound of running bath water drowned out her sobs. Now Papa's red brows furrowed as he drummed his fingers on the tablecloth.

Carl was shoveling cinnamon apples into his mouth and smirking. I felt the need to defend myself. Like somehow it was my fault. But all I could offer was, "The tire on their van was flat."

Mama flew back downstairs and grabbed my hand. A minute later I stood shivering in the nude, watching the stream rise, and waiting for the tub to fill.

I heard my parents in the hallway.

"I'll just run out there and change the tire—"

"Stan, no! You'll do no such thing."

"Barb, I've got plenty of tires at the shop."

"What, you'll give it to that…that thing, for free?"

I stepped into the scalding water and hid as much of myself as I could under the bubbles.

"Would you rather risk Ginny over a God-damned tire?"

The *slam* of the back door downstairs made the bathroom door rattle in its frame. Hearing Papa curse rattled me even more.

As I heard his tow truck pull away from our house, Mama shouting after him, I pictured Papa turning down that dead end road at night. How would it go for him? If the legends were true, those demon pets would come from the woods for him, while the Monstrum kids watched and salivated from shattered windows. But I knew Papa. He would go down fighting. I scrubbed until my skin was raw. In my mind, I saw myself on the bus, looking through the window at Papa's wrench swinging from the oak, the wind chime having taken on a much sadder tone. I scrubbed some more.

The water had turned cold and my fingers were pruned. Mama came in and towel-dried my hair. She was careful not to touch my skin. She rubbed the towel over my ears. But she couldn't drown out that sound. I slipped into a cotton nightgown, and peered out my bedroom window as the moon rose high. Papa's truck hadn't made its way back to our gravel drive. I fell asleep that night with the covers pulled tight and the sound of the wind chime in my ear.

The next morning, my dad's truck zoomed past the bus as we approached the dead end. When we pulled in front of the house, I saw the VW bus. No longer lopsided. The older Monstrums were piling into it, and the younger ones got on the bus. I'd been sitting alone. I guess Marla had decided to share her sour breath with some unfortunate sixth graders. I wasn't surprised. Mama had started painting her nails while I ate breakfast. As the butter melted on my pancakes, she apologized for not being able to give me a hug. Wet nails and all. I knew as the screen door slammed behind me, I'd be sitting alone on the bus today. Except for Eugene. He didn't hesitate. He sat down like he owned the seat.

Things went on like that for weeks. Mama tried to make me catch a ride with Carl and Scott, but there was no way I'd do that. The younger kids in town walked or rode their bikes to school. The bus picked up those of us on the outskirts of the county and dropped us off at "K through 8th" or the high school across campus. I was in eighth grade but Eugene continued to sit with me every day. And for some reason those blond twins with the conjoined braid kept riding the bus too, always sitting directly in front of us. I thought Eugene was five or six that day he dashed back into the house for God-knows-what. But he grew taller each day. He didn't shove. He didn't tease. He didn't talk about gross things boys generally talked about. In fact, he never talked at all. But he'd move to the aisle, and wait for me to exit first. With one look on the second day, he got every kid on the bus waiting for me to exit first.

It always seemed like Eugene's irises were looking ahead, but a second set behind them darted to the side for a split second if someone on the bus laughed or squealed or cried. Like he had one set of eyes to show to the world, and another he used to watch it. Sometimes when I giggled at my science teacher, or skinned my knee in gym, even if he wasn't in the same room,

I felt like those second irises were trying to fix on me. And on those rare occasions when I saw it, I couldn't tell if he was responding to emotion or trying to understand it.

I don't know how he got home in the afternoons. The twins rode the bus home, but I sat alone. I'd slide into our seat, and occasionally a surprise awaited me. A penny flattened by the 740 on the tracks. Half of a robin's egg he had to have kept since last spring, since before he'd even known me. A round dandelion weed with fluffy dreams just waiting to be blown onto the wind.

I'd tuck these treasures into a shoe box under my bed, slide into my cotton nightgown, and look out my window. Papa's truck was there in the moonlight, and his body roamed this house, but he'd never really come home after that night. Sometimes at dawn a barred owl would blend into the tree outside my window, its eyes watching me no matter which way I turned. Mama had stopped making excuses. We both knew hugs had gone by the wayside. I'd climb onto the bus. I'd fiddle with my pink plastic ring and pretend Eugene wasn't there. Pale as a ghost, silent as the grave, you'd almost think he wasn't. Except he was more *there*, more present, more aware, than anyone I'd ever known.

The only time I saw him at school was in the cafeteria. The Monstrum kids sat at their own lunch table under a "Class of '72!" homecoming banner. Apparently, they all had a food allergy. They brought sack lunches, but held the bags so close to their mouths, no one really knew what made those paper bags squirm.

One morning, the bus bounced over a rut and a drop of blood fell from Eugene's mouth onto his jeans.

"You're bleeding," I said. I heard the same concern in my voice my mom used to express for me.

He used his tongue to gingerly wiggle a tooth. Tears began to well in his eyes. I'd never seen him look frightened. That second set of irises darted about, terrified. I tried to reassure him.

"It's going to fall out. We all lose our baby teeth. It doesn't hurt."

The twins turned all the way around to face us. "Ginny, that's so cute." One licked her lips and the other traced one gloved finger over hers. Then they said in unison, their crystal-blue eyes mocking me, "It doesn't hurt to wose itty bitty baby teeth!" When they finished laughing, one said, "He's not afraid of the pain. Believe us. It hurts. But it's not teeth waiting to descend from his gums." They rested their chins on the back of the seat between us, and parted their lips ever so slightly. They waited until the bus was screeching to a halt to spring their jaws open so it would mask the sound of my scream.

In early November, for two weeks, Scott's mom called him in sick. Only we all knew the only kind of sick he had was waiting it out at juvie while Widow Hanks decided whether or not to press charges over her broken bay window and missing silver candlesticks. Without a ride to school, Carl was forced to walk the mile to our bus stop with me.

"Don't go thinking I'm going to sit with you."

I stopped, drawing a cold November wind into my lungs. No one sat with me. No one but Eugene. The thought that my brother didn't realize what was still going on was both a relief and a terror.

"You know how those weapons got there, don't you?" he said.

I remained silent. I'd heard the stories.

We'd stopped at the crossroads. The whistle of the 740 carried through the woods. I pulled my red wool hat down tighter over my ears.

"No one's ever killed a Monstrum. Not for lack of tryin'. But any weapon that strikes a blow will be taken as a warning. And the person who attacked them is never seen again." Carl said this with the smug arrogance of a man who knew it to his core. I turned away, but he droned on. "Papa's been warnin' me since I could walk. Their mama, she's a witch. Or a siren. Something like that. Turn even a good man bad. No doubt, the mom's got the dominant genes. Sure, they get the texture of their hair, the shape of their teeth, and their ungodly claws from their mother's side of the family. But have you ever noticed how that one's bushy unibrow looks just like Mr. Danner from the bank? He went out there in his Cadillac on a spring morning to foreclose on the house. Six years later they're still living in the house, and the kid's in middle school. And how about those twins? No one has eyes that blue and hair that white except for Parson Barkly. Nine years ago, he went there to consecrate the ground. And those girls look seventeen if they look a day."

I remembered that momentary glimpse those girls had shown me. Not wanting to harm me, just making sure I understood what was happening to Eugene. And that it would hurt.

I saw the puff of smoke over Gruber Hill and knew the bus would be here within a minute. The bus was as faithful as the train. I couldn't stand the thought of Carl seeing Eugene sit down with me. That look in my mother's eyes, or another shattered gravy boat. What caused my breakfast to rise in my throat was the thought of a fight breaking out between the two of them. What made me turn in my red plastic boots and walk the train tracks to school was the realization that I'd be rooting for Eugene.

A cold snap grabbed us just before school let out for the holidays and Papa made sure I bundled up. I'd pulled off my gloves and scarf and was putting things away in my locker when I overheard the fifth graders. That buck-toothed girl from the South side was sobbing as someone walked her down the hall. I felt someone bump me from behind. Scott towered over me and nodded toward the sobbing girl.

"It's a real shame. If she didn't want her bike to get stolen, she really should've put a lock on it." He took my hand and moved it toward his lips. "Have a lovely day, my dear."

I yanked my hand back. I slammed my locker shut. It was only after I'd walked down the hall and around the corner that I realized something was wrong. My hand felt empty.

"My ring." I said it to myself. I breathed it as softly as the wind on the window. I turned toward the sound of the sobs and watched the girl's friends comfort her. Eugene was at the end of the hall, but I saw his head whip around. I don't think he actually looked me in the eye. I think his gaze traced the tear as it ran down my cheek.

Between third and fourth period, I stopped by my locker.

The ring hung from the padlock. I put it on. I looked for Eugene in the gym. I looked for him in the cafeteria, and in the hallways. It was only as I peered out my window that night and saw the owl take flight that I realized something. Eugene's hands that morning on the bus. It was the first time I'd seen him wear gloves. Somehow I knew the cold couldn't touch him. He was changing.

We'd been back to school for over a week in January when a teacher asked me to take Eugene's homework to him. He hadn't shown up to school after the break. I started to ask why she didn't just give it to one of his siblings, but then she began stuttering and I took the folder.

I got off the bus past the dead end, aware of the eyes that watched me. My red boots crunched over the snow as I passed beneath the wind chime. I walked up the creaky steps. The screen door was closed but the main door was opened. Clearly, the cold didn't hurt them. I knocked.

Mother Monstrum came to the door, one hand on her belly.

Now I was the one stammering, but I didn't budge, even when a foot-long icicle dropped a few inches from me and shattered on the porch. "I'm Ginny. I've brought Eugene's homework."

She eyed me suspiciously. "You're that mechanic's kid." Her hand rubbed her belly. "Come on in."

I followed her into the house. It was the first time I'd seen her up close. Her gray hair was even longer than I'd realized. It trailed on the floor like a bridal veil as she moved ahead of me. It had picked up bits of leaves, dust, and dirt. When I saw beetles crawling through it, I felt my stomach churn. She turned to me, and in spite of that gray hair, she looked young. The only place I saw wrinkles was around her eyes. Her eyes looked so tired.

She took the homework assignment from my hand. She flipped the folder open and thumbed through the pages. The weariness in her voice matched her eyes when she spoke. "I had such high hopes for Eugene. But kids grow up so fast." She threw the folder in the cardboard box that passed as a trash can.

I looked out the kitchen window, and saw some of her kids out there. Mother Monstrum looked at me and shrugged her shoulders.

"Digging for dinner. I don't provide for my kids. It's all I can do to carry 'em in here for a few months." Her voice had softened a bit at that last statement. It seemed the only time she felt motherly was when they were inside her.

I heard melting snow shift on the roof, and water began to drip at a leaky spot in the kitchen.

"I need to get that fixed." She sounded so resigned. "I'll have to call a roofer." She paused and draped one arm across her belly. "But not yet."

No, of course not, I thought. *No use having a man out to the house when you've already got a bun in the oven.* Mama would wash my mouth out with soap if she knew I'd had such a thought. Still, I couldn't help but pity the roofer's wife.

Eugene's mother let out a small *"oh,"* just then. She set her gaze on me, and smiled. "Do you want to feel it kick?"

No. I don't want to feel it kick. I don't want to see it dig for grubs or wonder what comes in when its teeth fall out.

"Come on. You're a brave girl." She motioned me toward her.

I felt myself entranced. A part of me did want to feel it kick. She took my hand and placed it on the swell. I waited. Our breathing fell into a synchronized rhythm. Her old, wrinkly eyes smiled.

"There."

Whatever this creature would prove to be, whatever traits it inherited from its mother's line or its father's, right now, it was a miracle. Mother Monstrum nodded at my understanding.

"It's our blessing and our curse. The only time a woman knows exactly where her child is every moment. When they move. These months. After that, you do the best you can. A roof over their heads. But you have so little control…"

Through the warped window, I could see the shapes of her other children, gathering their dinner.

"That day," I said. "The first day Eugene rode the bus. What did he come back for?"

"A hug. From me. His first day of school. We can't...I can't, give them affection. Whatever warmth passes between us goes from them to me. I'm not a warm creature. I soak it up from whatever's around me. Eugene, he's said more with his eyes than scores of my kids have said with their lips. I've never heard Eugene speak. According to Gunther, he did say three words once." She paused. "In fact, it was that same day. He wanted that hug. That warmth passing between us. Because in the passing of an afternoon either of us might change, and he'd never feel it again. He wanted to remember. So that once he'd matured, there would still be a part of him, somewhere inside, that remembered what love's touch felt like."

She'd sounded melancholy as the melting snow dripped onto her cracked linoleum. "But I'm not a hugger." A brown tear welled in her eye but she brushed it away. "He never got what he deserved. My twins teased him about someone he wanted to hold hands with. Someone he'd given a ring to. But it's too late. He's gone to the woods now."

She grimaced and grabbed her belly. Something wet and warm ran down her leg. Her eyes carried three sets of irises when she growled at me.

"My water's broke, dear. You best head home. I get a little overprotective when I'm birthing." A swarm of cockroaches erupted from her hair and escaped to safety. I burst out the front door and heard the wind chime clanging behind me as I raced for the woods.

I only slowed once I got to the tracks. As I walked along, I sensed someone, or something, following me. At first, I thought I heard footsteps behind me in the woods. But soon the sound came from higher up. As though something were moving through the trees.

I was going to walk all the way home, but through the trees I could see lights on at Papa's shop. I was cold and exhausted and decided to get a ride home with Papa. But as I approached the back door, I realized the window had been smashed open and the door was ajar. I was about to run back toward the tracks when I heard a familiar giggle. I slipped inside the body shop. Carl stood there while his friend Scott loaded car batteries and tools into his car trunk.

"You can't do that," I said. Scott dropped something on his foot and cursed at me.

Carl's head whipped toward me and he immediately slumped his shoulders in defeat. He turned to Scott. "Man, it's over. Put it back."

Scott shook his head. "No way. You know how much green this stuff'll catch in Peoria? No eff-ing way."

Scott looked around and found a weapon of opportunity. Papa's wrench. He hefted it in his hands and a grin spread across his face.

I hated my brother. But to his credit, he stood up for me. "Dude, it's over." When Scott took a step toward me, Carl stepped between us. "Not worth it, man. That's my sister."

Scott used his practice swing on my brother. I heard a sick crunching sound as Carl's collarbone shattered and he dropped to the floor of the garage.

A '61 DeSoto sat nearby. It was on the lift dock but on the floor. I hit the switch and scrambled into the car. When Scott realized what I was doing, he swung the wrench at the car, but I continued to ascend. On the backswing, he smacked the chain of a bulb that began swinging wildly, casting dizzying shadows throughout the shop.

I peered out the window and realized something else had come in to the garage. A shadow. As the light bulb swung, I saw enormous wings. Scott swung the wrench, but claws grabbed it and snatched it away. Scott began screaming and kicking. He never realized his fatal mistake.

I don't know what happened to the rest of Scott's body, and I don't want to know. Maybe it was given a proper burial. Maybe it was scattered over the grubs and was the accompaniment to the Monstrum kids' next meal. But I know what happened to his foot. The one that became a weapon as soon as it struck out at the thing that came from the woods. My brother had to take the bus to school. He was afraid of me now but sat beside me. I know he saw Papa's wrench hanging from the wind chime as clearly as I did. Right next to that booted foot and ragged calf dangling from black laces. Some of the kids wondered why

Sheriff Graham didn't do anything about it. But I remembered that time he tried to serve a warrant to the old lady for back taxes. I saw the similarity between his cleft chin and Gunther's. And I knew why he ignored what hung from that tree.

It was that spring when I first saw the girl. The new runt of the V formation. Some of her siblings took after their fathers. And some went to the woods. I didn't know which side she would eventually favor. I saw her red hair, the red hair my mother always wished my brother or I would have inherited from our father.

She paused in the yard for a moment, but then continued toward the bus. Gunther was nowhere to be seen. The twins held the keys and strode toward the VW, but glanced my way and gave me a nod.

The girl was hesitant when she stepped into the aisle. There didn't seem to be a place for her. But I would make a place for her. I would leave my pink plastic ring on her padlock. When her eyes saw too much and the growing pains set in, I would tell her not to be afraid. I would hold her hand so she'd never forget. And if she went to the woods, I would walk the tracks just to keep her shadow company.

I turned to my brother and asked him to move. I'm pretty sure a second set of irises flicked when I said, "This seat's taken."

LIKE RIDING A BICYCLE

Morrison stared slack-jawed from behind his desk at the coffee stain. It was blurred around the edges. Café-au-lait colored. He knew that aside from that stain, the proposal was impeccable. No typos. Formatting was beautiful. Even the placement of the staple was aesthetically pleasing.

"*Look* at me when I'm talking to you," came the growl.

Morrison raised his eyes. Rich Dickie's imposing frame filled the doorway. Scarlet blotches had bloomed on the man's cheeks and were now spreading across his thick neck. On some level, Morrison was aware that his new boss was berating him, belittling him, and ordering him to provide a fresh copy of the proposal prior to the two o'clock board meeting. The floor vibrated as Mr. Dickie stomped away.

Morrison's gaze drifted back to the stain as it glared at him. Accusing him of sloppiness. *Slovenliness.* After he heard the door slam down the hall, he finally spoke out loud the words that had been swimming around his mind since the report had been flung onto his desk eight minutes ago. With only his pencil holder as a witness, he uttered his proclamation.

"But I don't even drink coffee."

"Second day on the job, and you've already managed to piss off the boss." The matronly woman from accounting pushed past him in the break room and reached into the freezer. She peeled the plastic off a portion of her meal, and popped the tray into the microwave. The crusty glass plate embarked on a lazy spin, uttering a distant hum.

What was her name? Beth? Bess?

"Someone must've reviewed the proposal without telling me," Morrison said, sounding more defensive than he wished. "I don't even drink coffee," he mumbled, gleaning a slight satisfaction from the fact that human ears had now heard his defense.

"Well, watch yourself. Jack Ziegler got fired a few months back for the same thing. Mr. Dickie's not a fan of slop."

The microwave pinged, and the woman moved her lunch onto the table. While she was distracted, mixing a gray blob of goo into a measly helping of mystery meat, Morrison stole a glance at the ID badge dangling from a frayed lanyard around her neck. *Becky Adkins.* They ate in silence. A couple of times he thought about making conversation, but she had such an absent, glazed look in her eyes, he didn't think it would be worth the effort. Come to think of it, that's how all the employees here seemed. Vacant. After Morrison finished his turkey on rye, he stood up from the table.

"What *is* that?" Becky asked, white plastic fork in mid-air. She was staring at his shirt, shooting a scolding glance at it.

Morrison glanced down. He'd worn a buttercream long-sleeved oxford with a royal blue and gold paisley tie. His jaw dropped when he saw the stain running in a diagonal across his torso. There was a nostalgic pattern to it, but he couldn't quite place it. He touched it, and a dark, oily, greasy smudge discolored his fingertips.

"My Lord," said Becky. "If I didn't know better, I'd say that looks like it came from a bike chain. You *do* know bikes aren't allowed around here, right? Not since Drew Beamer's fell over and ruined the new office carpet." She whistled. "Whoo-hoo, did Mr. Dickie ever have a cow over that one. Took it out of Drew's pay. Poor Drew. Now he's traded in twenty miles a day on his hybrid for a donut-laden train ride."

Morrison's mind was racing. He'd washed his hands right before coming to the break room. Surely he'd've noticed this in his reflection if it'd been there then. Blood rushed to his head, and all sound became a distant echo.

"... in your office." Becky was talking.

"What?" he asked, willing himself not to pass out. Her

mouth was full now, her jowls bouncing as she chewed. It seemed as though she were speaking in slow motion.

"I said, I hope you have a spare in your office." She laughed, sending gray droplets showering over the table.

The next morning, Morrison hung two fresh shirts and a new tie from the coat rack next to the silk fig tree behind his desk. Just in case.

He sat down and powered up his computer. He'd lain awake in the night, pondering how a coffee stain could appear on his report, and a bike chain track on his shirt. Around three a.m. he'd come to the conclusion that someone was trying to sabotage him. But who? And why?

At least no one can stain my emails, he thought as he read them and began sending responses. He was halfway through listening to his voice mails when that bony blonde from HR swooped into his office, her horse-shaped jaw yakking away.

"What were you thinking? Mr. Dickie is going to have your head on a platter over this." She shook her head, and as she began to walk out the door, he could practically see the thought balloons floating about her. *Disgusting. Completely disgusting.* She paused, resting one hand on the frame. "I never figured you for a porn guy. You seemed so *normal.*" There was a sense of betrayal in her eyes, like he'd made her a promise during the interview. *I'm always on time. I'm a people person. And I'm so normal.*

The increasingly familiar tightening of his chest sensation overcame him. *Porn?* Morrison's fingers hesitated as he searched for his sent emails. He scrolled through them.

7:57. Subject: Next Quarter's Projection. To: S.Levine@...

8:01. Subject: Brainstorming mtg pushed back to 11:30. To: A.Peters@..., M.Knoble@...

8:04. Subject: Fuzzy dice meet Tu-Lips. Who wants to play!!?? To: All@...

Don't click on the attachment. Do not *click on the attachment.* But his hand seemed to have found a mind of its own. The uber-megapixel detail would have been impressive had the image not been so utterly revolting as it unfurled across his monitor.

To: All.
All.
Everyone in the office. In his mind's eye he could imagine everyone in the firm opening the attachment. Even those who hadn't received the upgraded monitors would be in for quite a show. Big-bosomed Becky, playing with the strands of her lanyard, after placing her three-hundred calorie lunch in the freezer. Drew Beamer licking his donut-glazed fingertips as he leered at the fuzzy dice, leaving a glazy smudge on his cordless mouse. That red-headed vixen, Amy Mc'Something, would never agree to lunch with him now. And Mr. Dickie...

Morrison tried to delete it. Delete ALL. To take it back.

The screen politely disobeyed him. *Internet is not responding.* The little hourglass figure, sexy, sassy little vixen that she was, hovered. He could touch her, but he'd never reach her.

I've got to hide. Hide, and figure this out.

Morrison stepped into the hallway, the few people gathered there whispering conspiratorially, averting his gaze. He took the stairs two flights up, to the balcony. He kicked the cigarette urn, scaring away a few pigeons, and then gripped the railing. He was now seven stories above ground level. Traffic was slower now than at rush hour, but was still at a steady stream. He tightened his grip so much that his knuckles whitened. What to do?

Morrison leaned over, wondering if he would vomit. Pretty sure based on the clenching in his gut that he would. Imagining how his half-digested sunny-side-up egg and blueberry bagel would look splattering onto the heads of the pedestrians below. He knew this feeling. The helplessness. The anxiety. The hopelessness.

He watched people swarming in and out of the corner coffee shop. The barista was surely smiling. Cha-ching! He watched bike messengers and cycling commuters zipping up and down the street. An arm out to signal a turn. A helmeted head tucked to signal a speed burst. He watched for twenty minutes, but couldn't discern the signal for *I'm going to drop my chain across your shirt.* Can't shout that one out!

Morrison closed his eyes. His voice was pleading. "I don't drink coffee. I haven't ridden a bicycle since I was ten."

"And you've n-e-v-e-r looked at porn." The voice was in complete agreement with him.

He spun, and saw the waif-like girl looking over the railing about ten feet away. She was people-watching, her dark shaggy hair blowing in the breeze. "Although," she spoke, as though debating with herself, "Jack Ziegler drank coffee." She paused, squinting her eyes a bit, focusing on the coffee shop. "Got it from that place right down there. Every day. Extra crème. Always extra crème. Poor Jack couldn't stand anything bitter. He gave his heart and soul to this place. I tried to convince him to use a coaster, but..."

A sideways grin spread across her face and her gaze slid to Morrison. "I guess we both know how that worked out."

"But Ziegler was fired. What're you saying? That he snuck back in and damaged my report?"

The girl threw her head back and giggled.

"So you think he's in cahoots with Beamer?" She might as well have said, *Silly Boy*. "Beamer sold his bike in a garage sale. Needed the money to make up for what Dick Dickie was scalping from his check to pay for the carpet." She let that comment float between them for a moment. A few blocks away, someone honked their horn. Her voice was softer, less sarcastic when she spoke again. She tilted her head slightly forward, her dark gaze boring into him. "Beamer gave his soul to this place, too."

Morrison knew how they felt. He worked his first job out of college for nine years. Up the ladder. Was loyal. Did things right. Then his boss called him in one day, and patiently explained about the economy. How it had nothing to do with the quality of his work. How he was sure Morrison would bounce back and get scooped up right away.

"I'd given my heart and soul to that job," he whispered.

"I know." She stood, facing him now, one arm on the railing. Her eyes were beautiful. She understood.

"I found out, in the months following, he did it to a lot of us. Firing us before our ten years. Hiring in college grads for half the salary. It wasn't fair. We didn't do anything wrong." He moved closer to her, within arms' reach. "*I didn't do anything wrong.*"

"No," she said. Complete empathy rippled from her voice. "But you suffered. The pointless interviews. The disgrace of cashing those unemployment checks. And finally, two years later," her free arm swept over the building rooftop, "*this*."

"Someone's trying to sabotage me," he said, the desperation in his trembling voice palpable.

"No," she said, raising a delicate finger and hushing his lips. "Even they don't know it, but they are trying to warn you. Ziegler moved his family to Sandusky after getting a new job. I've no doubt he's leaving his coffee stains all along Lake Erie, from Toledo to Cleveland. He hasn't touched your report. But this place..." And at this, for the first time her confidence seemed to waiver. She shuddered, loathing thick in her voice, "this place sucks the spirit out of people. Jack's long gone, but his spirit remains."

"But Beamer," Morrison muttered, "he's still here. His office is four doors down from mine."

The girl's fawn-colored skirt fluttered in the breeze, revealing a tattooed anklet. She shook her head patiently. "Drew Beamer still comes to work, each week gaining another pound or two. But his spirit, his soul, belonged to the guy who did the Hilly Hundred six years running. He may be four doors down, but his spirit haunts this place."

He didn't want to accept it, but it was beginning to make sense. "If this place is so awful, that it drains the life and soul, what are you doing here?"

The waif smirked. "Dick Dickie caught me one morning. Thought I was alone with my vice." She bit her rosebud lip as though stifling something that wanted to fly free, but that she didn't want him to hear. "Anyway, I couldn't tell my parents I'd lost my first job. Especially since I'd lost it to porn. So, I ran up here, and jumped."

Morrison drew in a breath, looking her up and down. She looked so...unscathed. "Jumped? From here?" His gaze was drawn to the traffic seven stories below.

"My bad luck. Didn't realize the fruit vendor was delivering to the juice bar downstairs. The crates of mango and papaya in the bed of the truck broke my fall." She wavered. "Somewhat.

I'm in a coma, hooked up to a bunch of tubes in Mercy Hospital half a mile away." She seemed a little put out. "You know, I don't think those nurses have even washed my hair? My mom swears I still smell like a tropical smoothie every time she kisses my forehead."

Morrison looked across town. Past the quad apartments and the art district, he could see the hospital rising against the mid-morning sun.

"So what do I do?" he asked.

"What did you do last time?" She tugged on the hem of her sleeveless emerald lace shirt, a move that seemed modest for a girl who fancied fuzzy dice and tu-lips.

Morrison threw his hands into the air. "I spent about a year fantasizing about murdering my boss. All sorts of creative ways. Over and over." He looked at her, but saw no judgment in her dark eyes. "Then moved past the anger and depression. Eventually got this job. Was so excited, and incredibly nervous."

"Nervous because?"

"It had been a long time. But I got right back in the flow of it. I drew on my experience."

"Just like riding a bike," she said. She raised her eyebrows. "And those dreams you had over and over. The whole boss-killing scenario." Normally Morrison wasn't a fan of air quotes, but when she did them, they were kind of adorable. Especially when placed around *boss-killing scenario* and her lower lip got a little pouty. "You're pretty experienced at that, too?"

Morrison took a step back.

"No, that was just fantasy."

"So was you getting another job—until you got it." She crossed her arms in front of her. *So determined, for such a little thing.*

"But this is different, I couldn't begin to imagine—"

"Dicky Dickie always comes up to smoke a cigar after his ten o'clock constitutional." She looked at her vintage watch. "Which means he'll be here in about four minutes. And the fruit vendor won't pull up for at least another ten." She tossed a glance down the street. "Trust me, I know. Draw on all your experience. All your fantasies. You won't forget. You've done it before. I promise. It's just like riding a bicycle."

The fruit truck smashed into a light pole in its attempt to avoid the body, spilling everything from grapefruit to guava into three lanes. Morrison was surprised the next evening, strolling around the balcony at sunset, at the scent that still lingered in the air. And as he looked out over the shimmering skyline, he envied the waif's mother, who was able to smell the fruit smoothie with every kiss.

LUXOR DECANTED

I can't say with any sense of precision when a lark turned into obsession. I can, however, tell you the moment we first laid eyes upon the obelisk.

We arrived at the Louvre an hour before it opened. We'd inadvertently gotten off the Metro one stop too soon. Marlene had this mischievous grin as we raced for the museum, my hand tight in her grip. Entering the courtyard, she let go and ran forward. She turned, the early morning sunlight glinting off her light brown hair, and she beckoned me forward. *Come on, come on.* When I reached her, she flashed our museum passes in my face.

"See? Straight to the front of the line, just like I told you."

She leaned up onto her toes and kissed my cheek, then rested her head against my shoulder. I could feel her heart beating. I draped my arms around her waist and let my gaze wander. I saw it in the distance. The obelisk. It seemed a strange sight, in the heart of Paris. But then again, we were about to enter a pyramid. Sure, it was a glass pyramid. Marlene had told me about the urban legend. That it contained six hundred and sixty-six panes of glass. I felt tempted to start counting them, but there was too much else to look at. The architecture of the Louvre was impressive. Looking toward the obelisk, I could see the Eiffel Tower (or *la Tour Eiffel*, as Marlene had begun calling it) off to the left, and the Arc de Triomphe in the distance. We'd talked about this second honeymoon for years, and a part of me still couldn't believe we were actually here.

We spent the weekend following our wedding at her uncle's cabin in Kentucky. My rusted-out pickup got stuck in the weeds twice before we decided to walk the rest of the way. The only music in the cabin came from an old turntable and a stack of vinyl albums. Patsy Cline, Buddy Holly, Ritchie Valens type of stuff. That first night, on the rotted back porch, exchanging swigs from a bottle of Strawberry Hill, we pretended we were in Paris. Marlene pointed out the Eiffel Tower, cleverly disguised as a dying silver oak. I told her what looked like a mosquito-ridden crick was really the River Seine. The buzzing of the cicadas was actually the ringing of the bells of Notre Dame. There was a pause in the music as one album finished and another one dropped. The needle hit vinyl and through the open screen door I could hear the hiss and pop as it worked its way into the grooves.

As the lyrics of "You Belong to Me" serenaded us, describing pyramids along the Nile, I ran my hand up under the back of Marlene's tank top and pulled her close. She tasted like cheap, sweet wine, and I'd never been more in love with her.

Fireflies lit up the Champs-Élysées. As Marlene straddled me, her eyes a little glazed, and the rickety loveseat threatening to give out beneath us, I whispered to her about Paris.

As she unzipped my pants, I promised her I'd give her the world.

And now, ten years later, here we were. A group of local teens stood behind us. A man in a raincoat walked toward one of the fountains near the pyramid. He stood on the rim, hesitated, then stepped into the water. He kept his eyes down, as though he were searching for something. He shuffled, his stride through the water slow but steady. I hadn't remembered seeing fish in the pool of the fountain when we'd run past it, but something seemed to be swimming, or slithering, swirling, near his feet. The man finally looked up, looked around. Dazed. He seemed completely unaware of the hundreds in the courtyard, yet he *was* searching, for something.

"What do you make of that?" I asked. Marlene glanced up from her tour book and shrugged.

One of the teenagers behind us spoke up. "The Romani? Never mind him. He descended from the Italian Alps."

"Or arose from the depths of the Mediterranean, depending

on who's telling the tale," another one said.

The first one continued. "Anyway, he took up residence in the Tuileries, and developed Paris Syndrome."

"Paris Syndrome?" I'd never heard of it.

"Ah, *comment dis tu*, how do you say…hallu…hallucinations?"

Just then they began accepting visitors into the Louvre. The crowd moved forward and we descended beneath the pyramid. We didn't need to ask where the Mona Lisa was. Hordes of people were streaming toward the stairs. Just looking at that crowd made me claustrophobic. They brushed past me as though I weren't even there.

"Come on," Marlene said. I looked at the swarm of people and shook her off.

"You go. I'll wander around and meet you near the Venus de Milo."

I could tell she wanted to give me that disapproving look of hers for a longer period of time, but the swell was only growing, bottlenecking near the stairs. So she scurried off to see the lady.

I wandered, walking in the direction of the fewest people. Chatter faded until all I could hear was the sound of my own footfalls. I stopped in front of a marble bust of Osiris, and found myself staring into the cold, empty eyes of the god of the dead.

"Where have you been?"

I shook my head, and saw Marlene staring at me, her face a mixture of annoyance, embarrassment, and concern. I was no longer in the hallway with Osiris. I was in an alcove, standing on the wrong side of the velvet rope. My eyes focused, and I saw a crowd of people staring at me on display. I had one hand on a cold stone. I took a step back and realized it was an enormous sphinx.

"Come on," Marlene said, pulling me away. People gave me a wide berth.

"What happened to you?" she asked in a harsh whisper.

"Nothing," I said. I didn't know how I'd gotten there, or how long I'd stood there. How long had all those eyes been staring at me?

"You don't look good. I knew you should've eaten before we left this morning. Let's get lunch."

We emerged from the pyramid and walked toward the Tuileries. There was a fountain at the center of the garden. I couldn't help notice the wet footprints that led away, toward the Place de la Concorde.

"If we keep walking," Marlene said, "we'll get to the Champs-Élysées. There'll be plenty of cafés there."

As we got closer to the obelisk, I felt my heart racing. There was a buzzing in my ear. Then my wife's voice.

"On second thought, you sit. Rest. I'll grab something and bring lunch back."

I waited for some tourists to take a photo. Once they moved away, I walked up to the obelisk. I felt shaky, like I needed to steady myself. I raised my hand and leaned against the cool red granite. It was not long before I let my fingers trace the grooves of the hieroglyphics. Images of an Egyptian temple played throughout my mind. Then I heard a voice.

"Pardon, but I think you dropped this."

I looked. It was the man from the fountain. He held his hand toward me. In his fingers he clasped a golden ring that twinkled in the sunlight.

Instinctively I looked at my left hand. My wedding band was missing.

"She belongs to you. Take it," he insisted.

I felt guilty, worrying that Marlene would see that I'd lost it. I snatched it from him, and shoved it on my finger. It seemed tighter, biting down on me.

"You like the writing," he said, nodding toward the inscriptions on the stone. It wasn't a question.

Something dripped from the hem of his coat. It seemed too thick to be water. Then it slithered up his leg. "It's a shame it's here. The Luxor Obelisk. Ripped from the Luxor Temple, leaving its fraternal twin behind. Five years it took them. Ah, yes. Five years to build a ship shallow and narrow enough to navigate the Seine and the Nile, yet strong enough to survive the Mediterranean with the weight of the monolith she'd brought inside her. To sheath it, fell it, slide it into the ship, ride it over the swells and to erect it again."

This had very quickly turned into a one-sided conversation.

For a moment, the Romani seemed to be talking more to himself than to me. People had begun pointing at him again, and a little boy ran for the comfort of his mother's embrace. Enraged, the man was physically trembling as he continued his diatribe.

"The natives of Luxor swore the magic of the sun wouldn't allow them to tear it down. As the sun scorched them, those same men dug the trenches for the ship that would carry it away. And after the drunken French men defiled their virgin daughters, those same men beheaded their daughters out of shame. They tossed the heads into the Nile so the girls' eyes could look upward to watch this great phallus depart at the hands of their French lovers. So, five years it took the French. But this obelisk had stood there for *millennia*. With Egypt's dust in their lungs, those men swore The One would rise again and seek vengeance for this blasphemy." Sated, his anger seemed to dissipate for the moment, and he laughed. "You know what stood here before the Luxor Obelisk?"

I shook my head. The sun was rising higher, searing the images he'd described into my brain.

He laughed again, heartier this time, almost giddy. "The guillotine." He spread his arms out to the sides. "Heads rolled right where you are standing. Louis XVI. Marie-Antoinette. Three thousand others. They say the smell of the blood was so thick, even the horses refused to draw near."

The smell of copper thickened in the air. A falcon flew overhead, screeching, and my gut twisted, cramping. I felt moisture soaking into my socks. I tried to convince myself it was just sweat, but I couldn't shake the vision of my feet soaked in blood as heads rolled all around me.

"Did you know Dr. Guillotin was a pacifist? Abhorred the death penalty." He chuckled, but then his face took on a more serious countenance. "You want to thank Salvolini for the ring."

Hadn't I already said thank you? I couldn't remember.

"My people have a chateau along the Côte d'Azur," he said. "Still in France, but almost to the Italian border. They send me to Paris seeking guests. Everyone who visits the coast wants to see Cannes or Nice, Monte Carlo. But we have the most spectacular views of the Mediterranean in all of France. It's the top of the world."

"I don't know." My wedding band seemed to constrict even tighter. "We've got a hotel booked already. Nonrefundable."

"Then I don't charge you. We have a working vineyard. You do a small bit of labor in exchange. You will be our, *comment dis tu*, our 'word of mouth.' Also, you admire the hieroglyphs. You like history, I can show you more. We have our own Book of the Dead."

"I don't know. My wife—"

"Will be happy that the ring stays on your finger." He shoved a small card into my hand. "You want to thank Salvolini." It wasn't a question.

A few minutes later, Marlene came back with lunch. She raised a paper bag. "Croque Monsieur?" Of course she'd gotten mine without the ham. She was always thoughtful like that. The grilled cheese sandwich hit the spot. We sat on a bench while we ate, sunlight glinting off the pylon atop the obelisk.

"I know we planned to leave tomorrow for Normandy, but I've been thinking—"

"Uh oh," she said, giving me a skeptical look.

"We should go to the Côte d'Azur." I didn't want to seem too eager, but in reality I felt compelled to go regardless of her answer.

"The Riviera?" she said, still chewing a bite of her sandwich. She swallowed and wiped some Dijon from her lip. "I thought you hated that idea."

"I never hated it. I just wanted to find history. I met a guy who said his people have a place with the best views in the region." I took her hand. I did my best to remember the tune of that old doo-wop song and hummed a few bars.

Marlene giggled. "A tropic isle?"

I needed her to say yes so badly I could feel tears starting to sting my eyes. I kissed the back of her hand and whispered, "I still want to give you the world."

The next morning, we took the bullet train to Nice.

Marlene had fallen asleep about two hours into the train ride. We made quick time from Paris to Marseille, but then progress along the coast was slow as the train stopped in coastal town after town. I leaned over Marlene to get a better glimpse out the window. Vineyards stretched on for miles, and I wondered at all the wine, all the future headiness it was waiting to cause. Then I caught the first patch of blue. My head swam as though already drunk on wine, and my breath caught. There it was. The sea.

If Marlene had been awake, she'd have said the sunlight sparkled off it like diamonds. But it sparkled like scales. There was movement. There was life. And a more magnificent blue than I'd ever imagined.

We picked up a rental car after we got off the train in Nice. Marlene insisted on driving. I programmed the coordinates from the card into the GPS app on my phone. Soon, we were driving along the coastal highway. We veered seaward, then back toward the mountain over and over in a dizzying rhythm. Like a snake. Serpentine, serpentine.

I saw people on the beach, wading into the water. Splashing, oblivious to what might lie beneath. Houses dotted the mountainside. Some perched on cliffs.

My heart quickened as we neared our stop. "Turn here."

It was an impossible road. It veered up away from the highway, but seemed askew, as though the dimensions, the angle, didn't quite fit with the rest of reality. Marlene took the turn and something scraped along the bottom of the car. She let out a small yelp. The tires spun and dug in. I told her to downshift to get a better grip.

The drive was unfeasibly narrow as we ascended. On my side was a steep drop-off, on hers, the jagged rocky mountain. It scraped along her door more than once.

"This can't be right." I heard the fear in her voice, and somehow got satisfaction from it. "Are you a hundred percent sure? This just can't be right."

"I'm a thousand percent sure. We're almost there."

The car continued to climb. "There's got to be a place to turn around." Her voice was quivering.

We continued on for five minutes. Ten. Twenty. Marlene was trying to hold back the tears as her hands gripped the wheel tighter, and even I began to feel the suffocating pressure of my claustrophobia begin to close in as the road seemed to narrow even more.

"I'm not staying up here. We're switching hotels as soon—" A creature dropped onto the hood of the car. Marlene screamed and slammed on the brakes. The car veered toward the drop-off on my side, and the front tire left the road. I could feel it as that corner of the car dropped with a *thunk*, leaving the car listing badly. I looked at the animal and realized it was a baboon. It used its long shaggy arms to pound on the windshield, which began to crack under the pressure. The beast lunged its face forward and screeched at Marlene as its jaw seemed to come unhinged.

Marlene began hyperventilating, her wide eyes frozen on those long, curved, razor-sharp teeth. "I can't...breathe..."

"Get out of the car," I commanded.

She struggled for breath. "But the—"

The ring on my left hand squeezed my finger. "Get out!" The creature seemed to take an interest in me. At my dominance.

Marlene opened her door and scrambled out, tears streaming down her cheeks. I followed her, feeling the car shift beneath me. The creature scrambled up to the roof of the car and stood, screeching at us. I shoved the car, and it toppled over the edge. We heard the sound of angry metallic scraping and crunching. I could also hear the baboon screaming as it receded into the trees.

Marlene looked at me as though I'd gone mad.

"Why did you do that? Our luggage...my purse? The car!"

Annoyed, I responded. "You wanted to be rid of the baboon, didn't you?" She continued to look at me like I was crazy. I took a few paces, and then looked into her eyes, and softened my voice. "All of those things can be replaced." I approached her, and brushed my fingertips along her cheek. I meant it too. I could get through the rest of this without the luggage. Without the car. But I needed her. She must have seen that truth in my eyes. Marlene was still upset. She shook her head in that *what am I going to do with you?* gesture, but drew my hand from her cheek to her lips, closed her eyes, and kissed my palm.

We began walking up. Sweat was dripping down my back, my shirt clinging to me. My legs were aching, already strained from all the stair climbing we'd done that week.

Salvolini came around the corner.

"Ha! My friends. I was beginning to worry."

"We had a little trouble with the car," I said.

Marlene stopped and glared at me. "To put it mildly."

We climbed the rest of the way up the hill. Eventually, the path leveled out and opened into a courtyard. He stopped. Too exhausted to be polite, Marlene ignored him, walking into the entrance of the chateau.

The door was an open archway, letting in the warm summer breeze blowing up from the sea. The floor was made up of large flat stones. Marlene took her shoes off and walked across the room. She collapsed onto a couch.

"*Vin rouge?*" our host asked.

"Please," I said.

Marlene seemed in a daze. Shell-shocked. She hadn't even acknowledged Salvolini's question. I said, "Marlene, do you want some wine?"

She lifted her gaze and her eyes met mine. She nodded.

"Let us go to the cellar," Salvolini said.

"Be right back," I said to Marlene. She closed her eyes and settled more deeply into the couch. I followed our host.

He led me into a tunnel. It was dark at first, but with each step a light began to glow ahead of us. Motion sensor lights, I guessed, although I didn't see any bulbs or cords. The light glowed from crevasses off both sides of the tunnel. As we descended, the air became dry and cool.

I couldn't help noticing the writings along the walls of the cave.

"The Book of the Dead?" I asked.

"Yes. If you continue down, there is much more of it along the walls in the cavern. That is where our guests enjoy the grape stomping. I'll arrange everything in case you care to partake. After some nourishment, of course. Here," Salvolini said, his arm sweeping the air in front of hundreds of bottles. None of them were labeled.

"I'm really not an expert. Maybe you should choose."

"No. The grapes were stomped under the feet of previous guests. You choose. You will know the one."

I pulled one out. The bottle was huge. It had to hold at least four times as much as we were used to. We ascended and walked toward the kitchen. He opened the bottle.

"Soon, I will have everything prepared for you and your bride on the veranda. But first, we must transfer this to another vessel." Salvolini opened a cupboard, and pulled down a decanter, setting it on the counter. As he gingerly poured the wine from the bottle into the large glass carafe, he continued to speak. "This is a critical part of the process. The *most* critical. All of the work that has been done before—tending to the vines, harvesting and stomping the grapes, fermenting, storing it in darkness—it means nothing without decantation." He poured the last few worthy drops into the carafe. With a wide grin, he swirled what was left in the bottle in my direction. "Leaving the sediment, the bitterness, behind." In another one of those moments where I felt he was talking to himself rather than to me, he said, "And now, it needs to breathe."

I walked back into the foyer, where Marlene was pacing.

"I don't like it here."

"We've got the sea, wine, each other."

"You shoved our car over a cliff—"

"It was a rental car, and it's insured."

"We could just walk down the mountain." Still pacing, my wife was talking to the floor now. Chewing on a fingernail, she was mumbling, trying to convince herself. "Find another hotel. There's got to be some other place."

"Babe, we are both exhausted. It would be dark before we even made it to the base of the mountain. Let's rest up. Relax. Enjoy some wine and the view. I predict you're going to fall in love with this place. In the morning, if you're still able to tell me you want to leave, we leave."

I took her hand. She surrendered, and I led her to the veranda. A table awaited us. White table cloth. One plate of smoked salmon, and another of beef tartare. Two over-sized glasses of wine had already been poured.

"How did you—?" she began. "Never mind. I'm starving." I held her chair out for her and she took a seat.

We were well over a thousand feet above sea level, and had a view all the way to the horizon. Before I took a seat, I peered over the rail that ran part way along the veranda. I could see grapevines below, thick and twisted, and choking the hillside.

Marlene had never converted to my pescatarian diet. After I sat down, I watched as she broke the yoke of the raw egg that sat atop the raw minced beef. It was blood-red. She sprinkled capers, pepper, and finely chopped red onion over it, then drizzled the dish with olive oil.

I saw a flash of movement behind her and a golden jackal slunk out of the brush. It sniffed the air, smelling fresh meat. I stood with a fork in my hand, and growled. The jackal laid its ears back. One trembling lip curled up for a moment before it snuck away. I lowered my arm, and my stomach cramped as I sat back down.

I took a hunk of the fleshy pink salmon sprinkled with dill and plopped it into my mouth. It was so fresh, I began salivating. I could picture the fish when it had still been alive, swimming and darting across the current in the depths of the ocean. I pictured how it must've desperately attempted to avoid the net. How it must've suffocated when there was nothing to breathe but air. The dill tasted more like seaweed, but that only added to my enjoyment.

Marlene didn't say a word until she had finished half of her plate of beef, taking long, languid sips of wine after each bite. In her light blue sundress, she looked as though she belonged here.

She finally looked around to appreciate our surroundings. She reached up, and her fingers played with palm fronds that draped over her head. She finally realized there were palm trees all around. Where the railing ended, a long trough of water separated us from the drop-off, hundreds of pink flowers floating on the surface.

"Water lilies?" she asked.

"No, they're lotus flowers. See the rounded leaves?"

"They're beautiful."

I imagined Salvolini stepping out of the center of one of these at the bottom of the ocean.

Now on her third glass of wine, Marlene had a playful, tipsy look on her face. One bare foot began to rub against my ankle. She scootched her chair closer to mine and kissed me. She tasted of wine. Only this was no back-road Kentucky cabin wine. She tasted rich. Smooth. Full bodied.

"I've got a better use for those feet," I told her.

"Oh really?" she said. I filled her wineglass and lifted it.

I took Marlene by the hand and led her toward the tunnel. Again, those dim lights glowed as we passed down the corridor. We moved past the wine bottles, and descended further. The air grew even cooler, and Marlene ran one hand along her arm. Then there were stairs. Steep, carved stone steps descending into an abyss.

When it came to a platform, glowing firelight from torches shone around a throne-like chair. I set her glass down on a small table.

"My lady."

She sat, and I took her foot. I dipped a cloth into warm liquid. It smelled of incense. I ran the cloth slowly over her foot, her heel, her toes. I moved it up her calf and her muscles flexed, eliciting a small laugh from her. I could sense her breathing—shallow, anticipating. I took her other foot. I repeated the ritual, only more slowly. Torturously slow. There was no more giggling. Just an animal lust in her eyes. She was the queen, and I her slave.

I lifted her from the throne, not allowing her feet to touch the ground. I carried her toward the vat. I kissed her, her eyes reflecting the flames that danced all around us. I lifted her over the rim of the vat. Her arms clenched tighter around my neck.

"What the—"

"Grape stomping. We drank wine those before us stomped. Now we do the same in turn."

"It's work," she pouted.

"It's a privilege. Besides, everything involves sacrifice."

I brought her the wine glass, and she took another sip. "Now walk, my queen." I sang the first line of our song. The one about the pyramids.

Marlene took a tentative step. I could hear the fruit squishing beneath her, and the scent began to take over the room. At first she was squeamish, but the more she moved, the more she seemed to enjoy the sensation. She lifted the hem of her dress, but even so, it became soaked in red. She closed her eyes, and moved almost dance-like, swaying to a rhythm only she could hear. But she began to hum our song and in my mind I sang *you belong to me*. She passed by me and opened her eyes, holding her arms out to me to steady her.

"You know, when I saw you walking through that fountain, and then later leaning up against the sphinx, I thought you'd lost it. Especially when you jabbering to yourself near that obelisk and insisted we come here. But this is amazing."

"Me? In the *fountain*?"

The drumbeat sound of a heart began a distant hum. I thought back to that morning. Standing on the edge of the fountain, wanting to feel the water. Something swimming, slithering at my ankles. The kids pointing at me.

"How do you say...hallucinations?"

I remembered the ache I felt as the Luxor Obelisk passed fathoms overhead as it crossed the Mediterranean. How it had guarded the tomb of Ramses II who had waited for the return of The One. How I'd cried out as I tore and broke free from the lotus, slow-motion stomping across the sediment in the bed of the sea, always in the shadow of the ship far above me. The years I'd followed the obelisk, first on sea, then on land. Watched as they hoisted it up. Congratulated themselves on the location, not knowing it was the monolith itself who chose this spot. If it must remain in this foreign land, let it be in the heart of the blood bath.

I looked at my beautiful bride, in the heart of the bloodbath.

I could sense The One in the belly of the mountain. The falcon had come from the west and provided him intestines. The baboon from the north, breathing air into his lungs. The jackal from the east, providing his stomach and along with that a long-overdue hunger. It was gaining strength. All that was needed now to restore The One to its full power and glory was the human from the south to provide the wine-soaked liver.

I heard a roar and the rocky walls surrounding us shuddered as something began to slurp up from below. Marlene's eyes shone wide. To comfort her, I sang a few more lines from our song. I could tell by the way she gripped me, she couldn't understand why I was singing when the world was crashing down around us. "Sal? Get me out of here." She was pleading now.

Tentacles slithered out from my sleeves and pant legs. Out from *me*. I held her fast.

I could hear those doo-wop boys harmonizing in my mind as I sang one more line to her. It was hard singing and stifling a laugh at the same time.

The woman I'd been married to for ten years let out a scream then. But this wasn't your average "spider in the shower" scream. This was guttural. This, I'm quite certain, shredded pieces of her esophagus. This was sincere. I was so proud of her. And as that pride swelled in me, I reassured her.

"Straight to the front of the line, my love."

She struggled and shrieked some more, the sound echoing through the chamber and into the abyss. An even louder roar rose up to meet us. The walls trembled again and I could hear rock cracking, splintering. Dust fell from overhead. You'd think with all that, my claustrophobia would have reached its limits. But I'd never felt more liberated. Claws scraped along the rock floor and walls as euphoria enveloped me, and The One slithered forward. In the light of the torches, a thousand pulsing yellow eyes stared up at us. When it roared again, all I could think was that it put the baboon's teeth to shame. I'd never loved Marlene more than I did in that moment. I could have covered her mouth, but I liked the raspy sounds of her dust-filled screams.

HOUSING THE HOLLYGOBS

Tad scooped his hands under the cool, rushing water, but the minnows darted away in a shimmering rush.

"Cain't catch 'em like that. Need a net," Lynette said. At eight years old, her cousin was only a year younger than she was, but she said it with authority.

He tilted his head like a dog, blue eyes squinting under a shock of blond hair, and looked her in the eye. "Wasn't trying to catch them. Just playing."

They walked farther down the river, spotted a pencil-thin banded snake slithering among some stones, and then crossed a fallen log like it was a balance beam. Lynette knew it pretty well, knew where to step. It was Tad's first time, but he moved across it in his bare feet without hesitating.

They stopped for lunch. Lynette pulled two brisket sandwiches out of her pack and handed one to Tad.

"Aunt Karen's?" he asked.

Lynette nodded yes. Her mom was an amazing cook and Tad snatched the sandwich out of her outstretched hand. She divvied up the rest of the lunch: two large dill pickle spears, two crisp apples she'd picked herself, and homemade oatmeal cream pies. They washed it down with orange soda as the sun set lower in the sky over the hills to the west.

"So, the bonfire's tomorrow night?" Tad asked, pickle juice squirting from his mouth.

"Right," Lynette said.

"Cool," he said, his face growing more serious. "And then... Saturday."

"And then Saturday." Something splashed in the river, and

Lynette saw ripples on the surface. Lunch time for everyone. "That's when your folks are getting here?" she asked.

Tad took in a deep breath. "Yeah. Dad couldn't take off work. Do you think it's going to be weird?"

"Probably. Mom says everyone will say we've grown so much, and ask how school is going. And they'll bring so much food she won't have to cook for weeks. She says just to be polite. This isn't about us, it's about honoring Grandma."

Tad picked up a few flat stones and began skipping them on the water. "Was she...do you think she knew?"

Lynette thought about it for a moment, and then shook her head. "It was fast. We were picking apples two days before she went into the hospital." She noticed the stones. "You shouldn't throw those in the river. We can use those."

"Use them for what?"

She searched and found some flat stones. She grabbed wildflowers. She carefully pushed a little hill of dirt together. "So they don't get flooded out when it rains." She carefully placed the stones, forming a small structure, laid a piece of bark over the top, and decorated it with the petals. "There," she said, satisfied with her work. "Now you build one."

"Build one what?"

"A house. For the hollygobs."

"The holly-whats?"

"The hollygobs. The little people who live in the forest. Grandma says...*said*, they need shelter, and if you pass by and don't build a house, they'll steal your shoes in the night."

Tad looked down at his bare feet. "Mom's bringing my funeral shoes on Saturday. They've got nothing to steal tonight."

"But Grandma always said—"

"Grandma's not here." His voice was harsh but she could've sworn he was blinking back tears. He tossed the last of his rocks into the river. The first one skipped, but as he chucked them faster and with more anger, they just plopped and sank into the water.

He stomped off, stepping on the house she'd built. Her chest grew tight. This had always been a ritual, building homes for the hollygobs. Grandma's were beautiful, intricate, changing with the seasons. They never passed this way without leaving a shelter. Lynette thought of it more as a craft hobby they shared, but she loved hearing the stories of the hollygobs, and it seemed sacrilege to walk away without leaving a home. Like a betrayal to Grandma.

Blinking back her own tears now, Lynette searched for more stones and leaves and hastily built a lopsided shelter. She shouted after Tad, "Wait up." But she saw his blond hair bobbing as he jogged down the trail toward the farm. "I'm sorry," she whispered to the woods. "I promise the next one will be better."

They had baked beans and corn muffins for dinner. Then they went to the back field to catch fireflies.

"Do you put them in a jar?" Tad asked.

"No," Lynette said, "they'd die." She peeked through her clenched hands and saw the glow and then relaxed her hands, holding them up. The light blinked and flew away. On their way back, she plucked a bright yellow dandelion and slid it into the pocket of her overalls.

When they came inside, her mom saw Tad's mud-caked feet and insisted he take a bath before crawling into her clean sheets in the guest room. Lynette closed the door to her room behind her, and pulled the dandelion from her pocket. She slid off her shoes, and set them near the foot of her bed. She laid the dandelion inside one shoe, got into her pj's, and crawled into bed. A streak of lightning flashed in the distance, and a crack of thunder followed five seconds later. She thought of the hollygobs as she drifted toward sleep, and hoped her little lopsided house was keeping them dry.

Her mom made a large skillet of scrambled eggs with ham and onions for breakfast. Lynette was almost finished with hers when Tad shuffled into the room. Her mom looked up and asked, "How'd you sleep?"

Tad seemed a little dazed. He had dark circles under his eyes.

Lynette's mom tried again. "The storm keep you awake?"

"Yeah," he said, his gaze drifting toward the window. Tad sat down at the table, but just pushed the food around on his plate. The drizzle continued throughout the day. Lynette brought up boxes of crossword puzzles from the basement and laid them out on the dining room table. Mom had said they could work on them so long as they finished today. By tomorrow around noon they'd need that table for the feast all the people would bring.

Lynette offered to let Tad choose the puzzle. The boxes were old, the images faded and the cardboard bent or torn in places. "We've got A Dozen Puppies, Autumn Village, Scenic Landscape, or Sunken Ship."

She was sure he would choose Sunken Ship. It had a treasure chest, a shark, an octopus, and a skeleton pirate. He hesitated like he couldn't make up his mind, so she started to open the box to Sunken Ship.

"No," Tad said. He pulled Scenic Landscape closer to him, his fingers tracing along the river, and then to a dark copse of trees. He pulled the lid off and started looking for pieces.

They'd worked mostly in silence for about twenty minutes, finding the corners and the edges. Lynette was piecing together the clouds. Tad held one piece, completely black, in his fingers.

"What do the hollygobs look like?" His voice was low, somber.

She thought he was just trying to pass the time. Or maybe feel a little closer to Grandma.

"Well, no one's ever really seen one. They must be very little."

"Do you think they're always little?"

Lynette looked up from the clouds she'd been working on. She looked directly at Tad. "What do you mean?"

He hesitated, flipping the black puzzle piece over and over in his fingers.

"Something was in my room last night. That window won't shut tight because the wood is warped. I heard something scratching along the sill, and then drop to the floor. There was a clicking on the hardwood, like nails or claws. Like it was searching for something." He placed the puzzle piece in a shadowy section of woods, and looked up to meet her gaze. It almost seemed like he was trembling.

Lynette wasn't sure what to say. Tad wasn't used to being in the country. He seemed genuinely unsettled.

"We had mice two years ago," she said. "They'd come in when the temps were bitter cold. That scratching sound." She shuddered, remembering how she hated that sound.

"It wasn't a mouse." He placed a few more pieces. "I saw its shadow."

Lynette's dad walked in just then, asked if Tad could help him unload some of the extra chairs from his truck. Tad placed another piece of darkness in the center of the puzzle and walked out of the room to help her dad.

Lynette went upstairs into his room. She walked to the window and saw what he meant. It was warped, and there was a little crack. She placed her hand on the sill and swiped at the raindrops that had landed there. She could see something small like a wasp getting through there, but a mouse? Something even bigger? That was hard to imagine. She looked down and did see little muddy spots heading toward his bed. She knew the hollygobs weren't real, just some folklore Grandma had shared with her. But those spots on the floor, the sounds he described... *like it was searching for something*. Tad hadn't brought a pair of shoes. So, what would a hollygob take in its place? Lynette shook her head. She was being ridiculous.

The clouds had moved through by late afternoon, and that night at the bonfire, everyone roasted marshmallows. Dad and some of the other men threw old pallets onto the fire. The flames grew high and Tad cast a shadow, but it was much smaller than it should have been. To Lynette, it felt as though he was disappearing.

She went up to bed, but soon heard her door creak open. Something clicked across the room. Tad's voice came from the darkness. "Can I stay here? It's in my room again." Lynette scooted over and Tad slid under the covers. His body was cold and wet as though he'd spent the night outside in the elements. Lynette got out of bed to grab an extra blanket from the trunk near the window. When she turned back, she could see the slit of light under the door. A shadow moved along that slit of light, paused, and retreated. She tucked Tad in under the extra blanket, and listened to him shiver until he fell asleep.

In the morning, she went downstairs and found her mom making biscuits and gravy. Low voices drifted in from the sitting room. More relatives had already started showing up.

"Have you seen Tad?" Lynette asked.

Her mom held a wooden spoon and gestured with it toward the window. "Went for a walk a bit ago. I imagine he'll be back soon enough."

Lynette went out the back door, letting the porch screen door slam behind her. She raced down the trail and found Tad hunched over, gathering. He'd taken an empty grocery bag and was filling it with every good thing he could find. When he turned to look over his shoulder at Lynette, his eyes were hollow, his cheeks pale, his hair slicked to his head. His skin was hanging off his bones.

He stood, shaking, as though his legs could barely hold him. He reached into his bag and pulled out an empty snail shell. "Is this good?" he asked. He dropped that back into the bag and then held out a corn husk. "Do they like these?" Lynette was too stunned to answer, but Tad's voice became more desperate with each inquiry. He spied something, almost tripping as he went to reach for it, and then held a clump of moss out toward Lynette. "Will this keep them warm?" His voice cracked on that one. He was driven to take care of them, to shelter them.

Lynette took a step toward him, but he retreated, clutching the bag. He raced across the log spanning the river and lost his balance. The bag fell from his pinwheeling hands and splashed into the current. It was swept downstream, and disappeared around a bend.

Tad stood on the log, his face haunted as the forest enveloped him in shadow. Lynette stepped closer and realized he had faded to nothing.

She walked slowly into the house.

"Lynette, come greet everyone, and then you can help me set out some sweet tea," her mom said.

Lynette walked to the sitting room, saw a dozen or so

people. They were smiling sad, pitying smiles. She heard some whispers. "Poor thing. They were so close." She moved through them and went out the front door. Uncle Jim was unloading suitcases from the trunk of their car, and Aunt Deb was balancing a cake caddy in one hand while clutching a bouquet of daisies in the other.

"Do you have his funeral shoes?" Lynette asked.

"Why Lynette, you've grown so much since I've seen you," her aunt said.

"Tad's shoes. Do you have them?" Lynette tried to keep her voice steady, but she wanted to scream.

"Yes, what a dear you are, helping him get ready. They're in a blue shoebox in the trunk."

Lynette pushed past Uncle Jim, and saw the pale blue box in the corner of the car trunk. She took it and walked around the side of the house.

She sprinted down the path and set the box down alongside the river. Then she began to gather.

"Do you remember in springtime, Grandma always liked to use tulip tree petals for your window curtains? And buttercups in summer?"

The morning was already getting warm, humidity still in the air after the recent storms.

"Acorns in the fall, pinecones and holly berries in the winter. She made sure the structure was strong, taking her time finding the right stones. But she also sheltered you with love."

Lynette sat down and opened the lid of the box. A pair of brand-new, shiny black shoes gleamed at her. She lifted one out, the smell of new leather heavy in the air.

"This one is Tad's offer to you." She built up a little mound of dirt, and laid the shoe on its side, propping up the back with a large rock. She tucked some moss deep inside, and laid a large oak leaf over the top. She took a deep breath.

"And this one is mine." She placed his other new shoe in a similar fashion, inches from the first. She braided buttercups together and laid them near the opening to the shoe.

In the distance, Lynette heard a horn honking. More urgent, impatient. A while later she heard the church bells ringing. The service was starting. She took her time gathering and adding to the homes. Toadstools and a bird's feather to Tad's. A found butterfly wing and bright yellow dandelions to hers. When the bells rang again an hour later, she knew they would be lowering Grandma into the ground soon. But her place was here.

"This is Tad's. This is mine," she whispered to the silent woods. "We've taken good care of you. These shoes are so brand-new they'd have given him blisters today. Genuine leather. The Cadillac of hollygob homes. Take them both and give him back," she choked out, "or take us both."

The sun had long ago set. The fireflies were out. Lynette caught one and released it far into the depths of Tad's shoe. A glow emanated from the opening. As the moon rose in the east, something splashed in the river, almost masking the sound of whatever was moving steadily toward her through the woods.

THE FOURTH MOVEMENT

Mae sat straight up in the chair outside the principal's office. She always maintained better posture when she wore her marching band uniform. She had taken off her shako, her fingers tempted to play with the plume. She was determined not to cry. The window near the secretary's desk was open, rubbery autumn-themed window clings decorating the glass. She heard the sound of the buses' engines coming to life. Her friends in the alto sax section would be on the first bus, along with the other woodwinds, percussion, and drumline. High and low brass would be on the second bus, along with the color guard.

She heard muffled voices from beyond the door—the principal's low timbre, her mother's voice steady, but occasionally rising to a shrill, sharp beat. She couldn't make out the words, but she didn't need to. It was the tone that mattered.

The engines roared and the buses lurched out of the parking lot, going around the curve to cross the bridge. The kids in her section would hold their breath while crossing. Mae found herself holding her breath along with them. There was the sudden sound of crushing metal, and the first bus upended, falling off the bridge into the ravine below. The sound of brakes screamed across the football field as the second bus tried to stop, but the surface crumbled from underneath it and it plunged. A fireball erupted, followed by a billow of smoke rising from the canyon. Mae sensed the principal's door open, but kept her eyes on the smoke. When the explosion sounded and a second fireball rose up, she heard her mother's scream.

The accident had happened on a Friday morning. Mae didn't

leave the house on Saturday. Her mom tried to turn off the TV when Mae walked into the kitchen to get something to eat. Then Mae went back to her room, crawled under the covers, and watched the news on her laptop with her headphones in, drowning out the sound of rain against her window. As lightning flashed outside, the faces of her friends filled the screen, then faded. The tubas and flutes. Her sax section, she and Shar laughing. The drumline, Aaron the tallest in the middle, straps across his chest, drums resting just below his waist, drumsticks effortlessly in mid-beat. The crawl along the bottom described their most successful season yet, while the news anchors talked about infrastructure budgets, and how the bridge hadn't been kept up. Park rangers with canines had descended from a helicopter into the gorge to confirm that there were no survivors. The recent fall rains and mudslides made the supports unstable, the rotting wooden planks untenable. With high winds and more rain coming down, it wasn't safe to remove the wreckage. Or the bodies.

There was a voluntary convocation on Sunday. The principal reminded everyone how this had been the Marching Phoenix's best season yet. They'd swept all categories at Regionals. He shook his head as he blinked back a tear, and said again, almost under his breath, *All Categories*. They'd been on their way to the State Championship competition. Mae recalled the day they received the music for the fourth movement. She was in the sax section, but had been playing oboe since fifth grade, and they'd given her an oboe feature. When they got the drill, she realized she'd be playing while on a prop that would have her emerge from a cave while the others marched around her. The state competition would have been the first time an audience would have seen it performed in its entirety. Now, no one would ever see it.

She sat in a small row of chairs reserved for the four surviving members of the Marching Phoenix. Toby, a freshman trumpet player, cried, blinking back tears. He'd been sick on Friday. And since he'd moved to the school system halfway through summer band camp, he wasn't really a full member of the band. He was a hole-filler. There to shadow the other kids and learn the parts in case someone else couldn't perform. Jack, a senior drum major who had been in the mellophones until this year, was driving his car behind the buses when the accident happened. He would have stayed for the awards ceremony while the rest of the band headed home after competing. Now he just stared at his shoes. Red sneakers like hers. Like the ones Toby was wearing. Mae found herself angry with Jack. At his silence. She knew how close he'd been to Mr. Cripe, their band director. She knew Jack was in mourning. But he was supposed to be a leader, someone to look up to. Where were his perfect teeth, his words of inspiration? Even his perfect, thick black hair seemed to have lost its luster. Cynda, a junior in the color guard, had been out due to an injury. Today, she had her game face on, her hair pulled back in a thick, high ponytail. She was the only one who went to the microphone to say a few words when invited by the principal. She walked toward the podium on crutches, one ankle in a wrap, the other foot in a red sneaker, the skirt of her knee-length black dress swishing. A giant Phoenix painted on the cream-colored cinderblock wall rose up behind her, its red wings spread in triumph, beak pointed skyward.

"Of these sixty-seven kids, I'm sure every one of us has been asked, 'Why marching band? Why color guard? Why put yourself through all that?' Over the summer, while our friends are at the pool or the mall, we're on the blacktop for eleven hours straight. The band kids with their dot books, getting the drill, learning to march and find their place in an imaginary world. The guard, twirling our flags and rifles again and again, while the band kids weave in and out between us, striving for that perfect synchronization. We spend more time with each other than we do our own parents. Like any family, we break bread, courtesy of the spirit moms, we laugh, we get on each other's nerves. And like any family, we love each other." She closed her eyes for a moment, her dusky eye shadow shimmering under the lights of the gymnasium. Cynda cleared her throat, her long, thick lashes seeming damp when she looked over the audience. Her voice was strong and sure. "We start out as sixty-seven individuals. By the time we perform the show, we are one unit. We create something out of nothing. We move people and feel that energy, when we've left nothing on the field, palpable. We look around at each other, and without mouthing a word, we say with triumph in our eyes, *we did that.*" She turned to Mae and the others. "It's what we live for." She turned back to the audience. "It's what they died for." Her chest heaved and she declared, "We are the Marching Phoenix. And we will rise again."

On the drive home, Mae recalled Aaron's ex walking up to her in the parking lot. The redhead glared at her.

"When I found that photo of you on his phone, I shouldn't have shown it to the principal. You should have been on that bus."

Now Mae lay in bed, contemplating the fact that her continued existence was only thanks to the vengeful whims of someone she barely knew. The girl was right though. Mae should have been on that bus. She began to hear the music in her head. From the *knock knock knock* of the metronome, to the first notes of the first movement. In her room, her eyes were closed. In her mind, she was on the blacktop, her eyes glued to the two drum majors on their perches, white-gloved hands moving to direct the band. She thought about Aaron. About the hint of a smile on his lips as he walked away from her locker Friday morning. She thought about Shar's eyes as she saw Mae being pulled out of the line to load the buses heading to State. "You have to come right now," the school counselor had said. Shar's hands going palms up, eyes questioning her, *What is going on?*

"I'll catch up with you," Mae had said. Meaning *I'll be there in time for the performance.* She had to be. She was the solo feature. She'd repeated that to the counselor as they walked down the hall, and again to the principal as they waited for her mom to arrive. "I have to be there. They need me."

"We have a zero-tolerance policy. Suspension from extracurricular activities is a consequence."

She lay in her bed, and wondered why the secretary's window clings were on her window. They began crawling, falling to the floor. The smell coming through the window was the smell of worms after a rain, working their way to the surface to breathe. The smell of gasoline and smoke. The smell of the burning bodies of her friends. She was just drifting off to sleep when her phone buzzed. She had an incoming text. From Shar.

Monday after third period, she went up to Jack in the band hallway. "Have you heard from anyone since the accident?"

He hefted his backpack onto his shoulder and ignored her.

Mae persisted. "I know this sounds crazy, but last night, I got a text from Shar." It felt weird being in this almost empty hallway.

Jack met her eyes for a moment. "You're right. It sounds crazy."

Toby marched up to them. "Hey, guys?"

"Just a minute," Mae said.

"Guys, I went out on to the football field during lunch. I know I'm just a shadow, but I wanted to feel closer to them. And I found something."

Mae turned to Toby, and put a hand on his shoulder. "You are not just a shadow. Hold on a sec." She turned back to Jack. "I need to know if you've seen anything weird."

He shook his head and moved down the hallway to his locker. He spun the dial on the clunky lock to the right, to the left. "Weird like what?" Back again to the right, and he lifted the hinge.

When the door swung open, a rattling sound come from inside the locker. A charred, splintered drumstick tumbled out onto the floor and rolled toward his feet.

Mae stared at it, and felt Toby begin to tremble beneath her grip. She took a measured breath and softly said, "Weird like that."

Toby took quick strides, the sun peeking through dark clouds glinting off of his wiry auburn hair. Even though he was the shortest among them, they had to hurry to keep up.

They stood on the fifty-yard line, looking at a mud-streaked baritone case.

Cynda crossed the rain-soaked field using one crutch, and stopped a few yards back.

"Is this some kind of sick joke?"

Mae hesitated. "Someone left a charred drumstick inside Jack's locker. I got a text from Shar. Not a text really, just those little fading dots, repeating over and over. She's trying to tell me something. And Toby found this." She gestured at the case.

"Thanks for the shoes," Toby said to Cynda. Mae gave him a questioning look. He explained. "The red sneakers. My mom said they weren't respectful to wear to a convocation to remember...well—"

"Dead kids," Mae said.

"Yeah. So Cynda gave them to me in the hall right before we walked in." He turned to Cynda. "How did you know?"

"Little dude, I'm a badass with rifles and sabers. I have ways of knowing things." She winked at him. "By the way, are you skipping class to be here?" Her eyes moved up the hillside to the mansion perched toward the top. "Your momma's probably got binoculars on you right now."

"No. She's pulled all the curtains. Doesn't want to see the view again until—"

"Until they've removed the bodies," Cynda said.

Toby nodded and adjusted his glasses. "Sometimes at night, I go out on my balcony. I can see things down here—moving."

"You mean survivors? Mr. Cripe...the others?" Jack said, horrified and hopeful at the same time.

"No," Toby said. "They made sure. Nothing was moving on Friday. But now—"

Jack rolled his eyes and took a step back like he'd heard enough.

Toby went on. "I started using my drone to get some footage. The claw marks are getting higher every day. Like they are getting better with practice. Which is not surprising since they're marching band kids."

"Claw marks? What the hell are you even saying?" Jack yelled before storming off, toward the school.

Toby led Mae and Cynda, and they got as close to the ravine as they dared. Roots of lopsided trees clung impossibly to the hillside. Vultures swirled below, screeching. There was movement in the riverbed, and a red-tailed hawk swooped down, grasping the wriggling thing in its talons. As it soared over them, the hawk screamed and dropped its prey. The thing crawled toward them. Mae stood, transfixed, her mind trying to deny what was crawling toward her. A disembodied hand. Mae's screams echoed over the gorge as she felt arms drag her away.

"A hand?" Jack obviously didn't believe them.

"It wasn't just any hand," Mae said. "The fingers were moving. Like it was—"

"Like it was keying an instrument," Toby said. "Playing a song."

Kids started running past them. Teachers stepped into their doorways, peering down the hall. "What's going on?" one of them asked.

"Someone found the maintenance guy dead," a boy shouted.

They said he was found in the stadium stands, eyes wide open, and had bruises on his wrists and neck. Bruises that looked like hands had held him there.

Mae stopped to get gas on the way home, and saw Aaron's aunt alongside the next pump. She'd raised Aaron since he was four. It was obvious she'd been crying. Mae walked over to her.

"Are you ok? Do you want to come over to my house?" Mae asked.

"I can't stay. I think I'm losing my mind. Last night, I took a walk. I came up over the rise that overlooks the bridge. And in the dark, I could swear I saw those kids clawing their way up the ravine, instruments in tow. One of them came out of the scrub and grabbed me. Before I knew it, three or four of them had me, and started dragging me toward the stands." She rubbed her wrist, and Mae saw a hand-shaped bruise.

"I can't stay here. I'm leaving town."

Mae noticed something lying on the ledge near the rear car window. "Is that—"

Aaron's aunt reached into the car and retrieved the drumstick. "It was his." She held it out to Mae. "You keep it. I'm haunted enough."

"I think they're haunted," Mae said. "By the idea of not being able to play the fourth movement for an audience. I didn't even die, and *I'm* haunted about never being able to perform it." They sat on the balcony at Toby's house, no one quite looking out at the view. His mom had invited them over for dinner, thinking being around other band kids might help. She was inside cooking.

"Girl, they're never going to play it," Cynda said. She sighed and looked resigned. "They're never going to play anything again except maybe a harp at the Pearly Gates."

Jack was looking at the images from Toby's drone again, like he was trying to convince himself what he was seeing couldn't possibly be real.

Toby came out of the house holding a tray and used one hand to slide the glass door closed behind him. "Canapé?"

"They aren't at rest," Mae said. "Cynda, think about what you said at the convo. We groan about band camp. We live for the performance. For that feeling we get when we touch an audience with our music, with our movements. All through middle school I felt like I didn't belong anywhere. The Phoenix helped me figure out who I am. I need to do this for them. *We* need to. They learned the fourth movement and never got to perform it. That's why they are dragging people to the stands. I don't think they meant to kill anyone."

"Technically," Toby said, "they might not have killed anyone. The maintenance guy might have had a heart attack."

Mae shook her head. "The point is they need to perform the show. They need an audience."

They printed fliers Tuesday morning, advertising the memorial service for the Marching Phoenix that would take place that night. Mae convinced her mom to go with her. The field crew dads agreed to put out the props, turn on the spotlights, and hook up the mics. The assistant band director set up the met. It was obvious the adults were relieved to have something to do other than trying to figure out how to help these silent children.

Mae started the met and the loud *tick tick tick* boomed across the field. Jack was in uniform, but still didn't seem convinced.

"If you're right about this, that's like ringing the dinner bell," Jack said.

"I'm counting on it."

Cynda joined her on the field, her limp barely noticeable. She looked like a beautiful goblin.

Mae was nervous, but forced herself to speak. "Guys, there's something I need to tell you. About why I was in the principal's office. Why I wasn't on the bus."

Cars started pulling in to the parking lot as the moon rose low over the hillside. Parents and students began to fill the stands. This wasn't the raucous group that she'd experienced at football games. This was a somber, grieving crowd.

Cynda asked, "Did you kill anyone?"

"No, of course not," Mae said.

"Is it going to happen again?"

Mae hesitated, thinking of Aaron, and that hint of a smile. "No."

"Then it doesn't matter. It's showtime."

Toby took his place on the thirty-yard line and waited.

Mae heard the steady *tick tick* of the met, and then another sound joined it. A whispered chant—

Push one two four six eight...push one two four six eight...

Mae turned, and saw them stumbling toward her. At first the chanting was disjointed, but as they got closer, they fell into a rhythm. Some cries and screams erupted from the stands as audience members realized what they were seeing, and a few people fled to their cars, peeling away before their doors had even slammed shut. But most, possibly out of pure shock, remained.

The smell of rotting burnt flesh drifted across the field. The dead marched forth. Their black uniforms each had a red sash. The fiery red plumes of most of the shakos were singed or burnt away entirely. Mae approached Aaron in the drumline. He was burnt and broken, but he didn't know it. She placed the drumsticks in his hands.

As each of the kids took their place on the field, the band director shambled toward the mic. He tried to talk, but his vocal chords had been burnt away. This man had been a father figure to Jack. Jack hadn't believed Mae's theory. Hadn't believed that the Phoenix would rise tonight. But here they were, with the man who taught Jack how to be a leader trying to speak but unable to find his voice. While Mr. Cripe gestured to the band, Jack spoke for him, his words of inspiration echoing across the field with just the right pitch and inflection.

A dead parent, one of the chaperones, climbed into the stands and sat next to Mae's mom.

Jack climbed to the top of the perch and removed his shako. He turned to the crowd, gestured with his hand, and turned to the band. The band director stopped the met and the field fell quiet.

The first movement began slowly, a guard girl in a dress walking through the forest. Gnomes peeked from behind trees and swung from branches. The sax section started out lying down, but quickly moved into a tight formation. Mae could hear the trumpets coming from the corner of the field behind her and thought of Toby.

She'd assumed with missing fingers, shattered bones, and no air in their lungs, that her bandmates wouldn't actually be able to create sound. But they did. The sound was as perfect as she'd ever heard. It wasn't their physical forms creating the sound in this moment. It was muscle memory of the soul.

As the third movement wound down to an end, Mae removed her shako, exchanged her sax for her oboe, and climbed onto the rolling prop. She emerged from a cave, her notes guiding the lost girl into the hall of the Mountain King who sat on his throne, holding his scepter. The baritones and flutes began to circle her closer and closer, the drumline rushed toward her, faster and tighter as the mallets in percussion pounded. Mae's mom rose to her feet in the audience, worry on her face. The dead chaperone gripped her by the wrist. Mae commanded her to sit back down with her eyes, and her mother acquiesced.

Mae finished her feature and sank back into the darkness of the cave. She felt the guard rolling her prop off the field before they raced back to the formation. The music was intentionally discordant and frenetic until the last two measures when they synced in harmony. Mae stepped out of the darkness just in time to watch the large silk tarp flow, billowing and enshrouding the band, as the last note faded.

A hush fell over the scene. There was a little movement under the tarp and Cynda crawled out. She looked at Mae standing near the prop and at Jack up on his perch, and mouthed "Toby?"

Jack joined them on the field and they all pulled on the billowy tarp, frantically bundling it as they went. The wind picked up, carrying swirls of fine ash toward the ravine. Instruments were strewn across the field, but the perished students had vanished. Toby sat among the trumpets. He was stoic for a moment, then smiled, triumphant, as a tear ran down his face.

Thunderous applause erupted from the stands. The woman next to Mae's mom dissipated into the wind while clapping, a look of pure bliss on her face.

Mae offered her hand to Toby, and helped pull him up.

"Am I still a shadow? Do I get to hear the story of the first Phoenix?" The story the freshman heard whispered hints about all season. The story they would hear on the bus on the way back from their last competition every season. An urban legend about the first Phoenix.

"No. You're going to hear something better." As the moon rose over the valley, Mae put her arm around his shoulders and walked him toward the bridge. "You're going to help us find ways and moments to hint about it around the new kids next year." Jack supported Cynda, whose limp was more pronounced, and the four of them stopped.

Mae said, "We'll be a small but mighty group. And on the last day you'll tell them the story about how sixty-seven kids came together on a cool autumn night, and how the Marching Phoenix rose again." She wasn't sure if it was memory or imagination. Or perhaps the last reverberation of the final movement. But she thought she heard the faintest sound of the wheels of a bus crossing ghost planks. She held her breath for a measure or two, and then smiled because she knew they'd made it to the other side.

'NEATH FALLOW GROUND

Rand Gallaher left the southern hills and lowlands of Indiana behind him as he drove. Accustomed to the forested banks and rolling hills of the Ohio River Valley, he'd forgotten how flat everything seemed in the northern part of the state. The air conditioning in his rusted compact hadn't worked since he bought it a year ago from a used-car dealer in New Albany. Uncle Phil had promised him, if he'd had no tickets and no accidents by the time he turned seventeen, he'd go fifty-fifty on the car. Phil had kept his word. So the window was rolled down, and Rand let the humid July air whip through his hair as he cruised down the highway.

He passed signs for Fairmount and saw a billboard of James Dean. If he stayed on I-69, he'd eventually come to Fort Wayne. But he wouldn't be going that far. His grandparents' place was in that big stretch of nowhere between Wabash and Bluffton. Farm country.

Soybean and corn fields flanked the road. Each farm had the house plopped out in the middle of the property. Usually one shade tree out in the field, where the farmer could enjoy his lunch, and get a little respite from the blistering heat of the day. Rand recalled the summer days he'd spent with Grandpa under their shade tree, surrounded by headstones, chasing down egg salad sandwiches with strawberry lemonade. Then when he turned twelve, he'd been sent without explanation to New Albany to live with Uncle Phil.

The monotony of the drive was broken by the occasional group of running horses or cud-chewing cows behind rickety wire-and-post fences. The scents changed by the mile. The distinctive smell of a pig farm. The grainy smell of the field. Every now and then Rand would see roadkill on the shoulder of the highway. Coons and opossums mostly. As he got closer to his grandparents' place, he noticed the trees. By this time of summer, they should have been full-leaved. But as he drew nearer his birthplace, the trees looked shrunken, sickly. The hickories, the white oak, everything. Almost like a blight had swept through here.

Sweat dripped down his temples as he turned off the highway onto a two-lane dirt road that led to the farm. Movement at the center of the dash suddenly caught his eye. Something crawled up out of the vent and whizzed toward his head, making a clicking and chittering sound as it went. Rand batted at it, and slowed his car, seeing the dust cloud his tires kicked up in his rearview mirror. He pulled off in front of a roadside vegetable stand.

The thing was darting back and forth, dive-bombing for his face. Rand fumbled with his door handle and stumbled out of the car. *Dammit*. When he'd stopped for gas earlier, he'd seen a swarm of the bugs. Didn't know what they were. Most flew in a thick cloud, but hundreds lay on the ground, crunching under his tires as he pulled in the lot, and under his boots as he walked up to the window to pay for the gas. And they were loud as hell.

When he'd prepared to pull back onto the highway, a few were buzzing around in his car. He used a map to shoo them out the window. He must've missed one. Rand was fearless when it came to four-wheeling, jumping off bridges into the Ohio, or even flirting with a pretty girl. But the one thing he hated was bugs.

Now, standing roadside, he brushed his hands up and down his shirt and jeans, and shook his hair, making sure the thing wasn't clinging to him. He sensed someone watching him, and looked up to see a girl on the other side of the vegetable stand. Her hair was the golden color of corn silk. She barely looked old enough to go to senior prom. Damned if she didn't have a grin on her face.

"Something funny?" he asked. He shook his long brown bangs out of his face.

"I've just never seen a grown man so afraid of a little cicada, that's all."

Cicada. "So that's what they are? Are they dangerous?"

"Not these. You can make out letters of the alphabet on their wings if you look close. And these make love in a harmless way."

"What do you mean?" Rand asked. Maybe it was the way she seemed slightly superior to him. Or that golden corn silk hair of hers. But in spite of himself, he was curious. Besides, there didn't seem to be anyone else for miles, and she seemed lonely for conversation.

"Well," she said, standing in front of a table of home-baked pies, "the nymphs emerge from the ground at over a million per acre, after feeding on the fluid of tree roots on their way to the surface. They molt out of their exoskeleton and sing their song." She said *sing their song* like it was the most romantic thing in the world. She sounded almost wistful when she went on. "The males use their tymbals, the females a wing flick. They say the chorus can be deafening. Over a hundred decibels."

Rand played bass guitar in a band. He knew that was as loud as standing right next to the speaker at a rock concert. *Permanent hearing loss,* as Uncle Phil had told him a gazillion times. The girl's expression turned more serious.

"After mating, the female cuts V-shaped slits in the bark of young or weak live twigs. Then she lays hundreds of eggs."

"Why the sad face?" he asked, moving in closer to step into the shade of the stand.

"I feel sorry for the twig. It's not its fault that it's young or weak." There was an awkward pause, and then she asked if he'd like anything.

"I'll take half a dozen ears of the sweet corn, a pint of blueberries, and a loaf of the banana nut bread." Maybe Grandpa wouldn't be so angry when he showed up if he had a peace offering in hand. And if Grandma was as sick as Uncle Phil made out, he was sure there hadn't been any home-baked goods in their kitchen all summer.

When she bent and reached, he saw bruising just below the hem of her too-short jean shorts. When she leaned forward to grab the berries, he caught a glimpse of a pink bra and the swell of her breast beneath her white tank top. The girl stood and smiled at him.

"Do I know you from somewhere?" he asked.

"Darby Swanson," she said. She began to hand him his sack, but nearly dropped it. He figured her arms were fatigued from lifting all these crops.

A hazy memory swam to the surface of his mind. A little girl, with big blue eyes and corn silk hair. Peeking around the corner as her father set Rand's arm in a cast.

"Doc Swanson's daughter?"

"The one and only. And you are?"

"Rand Gallaher. My grandparents live just up the road."

Her blue eyes suddenly looked a shade darker. Her smile disappeared. She looked up the road. Her gaze and tone were letting him know he was unwelcome.

"I hear they left town. You might as well turn around and go back where you came from." He couldn't figure out why she was lying, but he knew as sick as Grandma was, they'd never leave town.

Rand took his sack of goods, jumped in his car, and headed for the farm. As the sun set behind him, he didn't mind the wake of dust his tires kicked up. A part of him hoped the girl would choke on it.

He pulled his car into the long gravel drive about ten minutes later. He thought about walking right in the front door, but didn't want to startle anyone, so he rang the bell. Through lace curtains, he saw a shuffling figure make its way toward him. When his grandfather looked upon him with his soft brown eyes, his gaze was a mixture of hopeful recognition and dread.

"Randall?" the old man croaked.

"Grandpa," he breathed. He dropped his duffle bag and threw his arms around him. All thoughts of the practiced speech flew out of his head. His resentment at being banished for unknown reasons, his angst over how he would fit back in. It all dissipated into the hot July afternoon with that one long, lingering embrace.

But Grandpa wouldn't quite let him in the door.

"Randall." There was so much in his tone of voice, so much in the look on his face. An apology, a warning, more. "This isn't a good time."

Rand tried to respond with an equal determination. "Uncle Phil told me Grandma's dying. I aim to see her." Yesterday he would've said, "I'm going to see her." Even he didn't think he'd ever used the word *aim* in that manner. But here it felt right. Sounded right, and just might get him in the door. Funny how a person could fall back into a certain kind of speak when among kin.

"Come on in," Grandpa said. In the kitchen, Rand dropped the paper bag onto the kitchen counter. He lifted out the blueberries and the corn. He set the loaf of banana nut bread on the kitchen table. His grandpa's eyes lifted toward the stairs, and gazed upward. "She's in bad shape, boy. Don't know that she'll recognize you." Almost like he was trying to convince himself, the old man went on. "Guess there's no harm in you goin' up there."

Rand climbed the stairs. He led himself to what used to be his room. He ducked to avoid hitting his lanky six-foot frame on the slanted ceiling. He dropped his duffle bag in the corner, and then opened the cedar chest at the foot of the bed. The smell of mothballs engulfed him as he lifted the hand-quilted bedspread out of the chest and laid it across the bed. He went to the window, tempted to open it. But there would be no cool breeze of the Ohio River blowing in tonight. He was upland, and only the thick, close air of an Indiana farmland summer was out there waiting to greet him.

He heard voices through the floor vent, as he'd done as a child. He recognized Grandpa's voice.

"Do you think she'll make it through the night?"

A bumping sound, floorboards creaking.

"I don't know. I've set her up with a morphine drip to help with the pain. So long as I keep the dose low enough, she should see tomorrow." More fumbling noises. "Is this Darby's bread?"

"I don't know," Grandpa said, uninterested. "Rand brought it by."

"She's got a full scholarship to Purdue. She can't leave here soon enough to suit me."

He was crunched down low, listening to the hollow tone of their voices as they were carried through the vent. Rand heard the porch door swing open and slam shut. Then another voice joined the conversation downstairs. *Darby?* Her dad must've picked her up at the roadside stand before coming over here to check on Grandma. He stood up straight, and looked through the doorway down the hall. Rand walked toward his grandmother's bedroom.

An antiseptic smell, trying to mask the deeper odor of decaying flesh, hit his nose as he walked into the room. Grandma lay in the bed, hooked up to tubes and fluids. Her skin looked so shrunken. As though it had been struck by a blight. She'd always been hard of hearing out of her right ear, so Rand moved around to her left, and knelt by her bedside.

"Grandma? It's me, Randall."

Her jaw hung open, slack. Her eyelids were at half-mast, unfocused. *She looks worse than Uncle Phil described.* But her head turned toward him. Her hand, covered in paper-thin skin, scooted across the yellowed floral-print sheet in his direction. *She knows I'm here.*

He reached over and held her hand in his. He leaned down and kissed her forehead. She smelled old, yet familiar. Her lips moved slightly, but no sound came out. He bent down toward her good ear.

"I love you, Gran. I've always loved you."

He began humming a song she used to sing to him at bedtime. It was from an old 45 record he played on his toy record player, from a Mary's Little Lamb song. It was sweet, but sad and haunting at the same time. It described the point where they were saying goodnight to each other. And also goodbye. Her head nodded subtly from side to side in time with the rhythm of the lullaby.

When the song was over, she fussed with the needle poking into the inner crook of her elbow. Then suddenly, she clenched her stomach, and a horrible sound erupted from her throat. Her face was contorted in pain. Doc Swanson's words reverberated in his mind. *So long as I keep the dose low enough, she should see tomorrow.*

His first memories were of this woman. Her arms around him, her voice reading to him. Her eyes smiling at him. When he was hurt, she always made it better. It ripped him apart to hear her in torment.

"Don't worry, Grandma, I'm here." His throat felt thick as he reached for the morphine drip. He hesitated for a moment, one part of his mind screaming at him to stop. But she was suffering, and he was in a position to ease her pain. He turned the drip up. At first she seemed to protest, but then she lay still, letting him stroke her cheek, and hum his lullaby. As the death rattle shuddered in her chest and escaped her lips, Rand heard heavy footsteps coming up the stairs.

His grandfather walked in the room, and came to the side of the bed.

Grandpa turned her face, but her lifeless eyes wouldn't meet his gaze. He spun on Rand.

"What did you do?" he growled. Doc Swanson rushed to her bedside, yanking the IV out of her arm. No blood leaked from the insertion site. Her heart must've stopped pumping. The doctor yelled downstairs at Darby to bring his medical bag from the truck. He began chest compressions and was pushing so hard Rand heard a loud *crack* as his grandmother's ribs broke.

"She was suffering—" Rand tried to explain.

"Bring her back!" Grandpa yelled. It was clear the doc was desperate to do just that. Darby ran in with his open bag. The doc plunged his hand in, and readied a needle with a clear liquid from a vial. He punched it into Grandma's chest and waited. There was no response.

Grandpa looked directly at Rand. His entire face was filled with a rage so all-encompassing, for the first time in his life, Rand was actually afraid of his own grandfather.

"Get out," Grandpa commanded. Then as loud as his octogenarian vocal chords could tolerate, he screamed it. "Get out!"

Rand scampered down the stairs. He could hear someone following behind him. He burst through the screen door, letting it slam and bang shut behind him, but heard it squeak as it swung open again. The humidity hit him, and sweat dotted his forehead. He ran behind the farmhouse and collapsed on the ground, leaning against one of the old logs that encircled their campfire site. If this had been a chilly fall night, they'd have a roaring fire at the center of these logs. As it was, just dead ashes from a night long ago were there. Thinking that tonight, everything but the cicadas seemed dead, Rand dropped his head onto his knees and wept.

Darby sat down beside him. The rhythmic sound of the cicadas surrounded the adjacent pond. Rand felt a gentle hand stroking across his back. He didn't know how much time passed. Rand thinking of Grandma humming a lullaby. Darby's magic fingers stroking his back. And always the cicadas played on. But eventually, he heard footsteps nearing the fire pit.

He heard a large inhale and exhale of breath before his grandpa spoke.

"Sit up, boy. There's some things I've got to say to you."

Rand wiped his eyes. He saw his grandpa and Doc Swanson. Each took a seat on separate logs facing the dead fire pit. Rand and Darby did the same. Grandpa looked around slowly, toward the farmhouse, to the lighted upper window, then out across and beyond the pond.

"You know, this is the richest land in the country. The Tipton Till Plains. Back from when the poles were reversed, millions of years ago, glaciers moved through here like a steamroller. Flattened everything and carried the till. A mixture of soil and rocks. Later, for thousands of years, this was all grassland. The grasses would grow, die, and put nutrients back into the ground. That's why we still let it lie fallow on occasion. We've got over six feet of topsoil here. You won't find that anywhere else in the world."

Rand had heard all this before, but he figured he'd just killed the man's wife. If it made Grandpa feel better to talk about farming, Rand would listen to him until the cows came home. Something splashed in the pond. Probably a bullfrog. Rand looked up at the night sky. It was a different sky than the one he'd seen for the past six years. Here you could see each and every little star, bright and twinkling against black velvet. When he was younger, he'd even seen comets and shooting stars while sitting in this same spot. Heck, sitting here, you could see the entire blasted Milky Way.

"Yep," Grandpa continued. "The glaciers brung the till. But they brung something else, too." The symphony of cicadas was constant and ringing in the humid night air. "Rand, something got buried. Got buried deep. Must've lain dormant a long time, but something shook it loose. Maybe a tremor along the New Madrid fault. Doc here says some scientists proved there was a series of large quakes around 2350 B.C." Grandpa shook his head. "To think, them beasts have been clawing their way out of the earth, all the way to the surface every seventeen years for over four thousand years."

Rand looked at Darby and her father and wondered why neither of them were looking at Grandpa like he was crazy.

"Are you talking about the cicadas?" Rand asked.

"These cicadas? No. But there's thousands of species of cicadas. One thing they all have in common is they erupt in a cycle of prime numbers. Thirteen years, or seventeen years, you know? Doc calls it 'predator satiation.' The ones I'm talking about, they ain't like any local bug I ever seen. I think they traveled a helluva long way. They say these kind of bugs can survive anything. A nuclear blast, an Ice Age. A ride on a meteor across the Milky Way." His grandpa stood up, slow, letting his knees adjust to a standing position. "Walk with me."

Rand stood and followed as his grandfather walked around the pond, toward the small cemetery plot beneath the shade tree in the middle of their field. The tree looked healthy, in spite of the blight.

"What kind of tree is that?" Rand asked, genuinely curious, and also trying to break the silence.

"Black Gum. *Nyssa Sylvatica*. Means 'Water Nymph of the Woods.'" His grandpa looked the tree up and down, and then looked way down, as though he could see what lie beneath. "It's got fleshy roots." His grandfather spit, then directed Rand's attention to the gravesites. He handed him a flashlight.

"You ever look close at these? This is where your grandma was supposed to be buried."

Rand accepted the flashlight, and casually held the beam toward the headstones.

"Grandpa, I can help you with that in the morning."

"No," he yelled. Then his voice grew softer. "She can't be buried here now."

Rand didn't question why. It didn't seem wise at the moment. But then he began to notice something. The date of death, on all the tombstones. It was the same date, just seventeen years apart. Even his own mother, the most recent one, seventeen years ago.

"Grandpa," he said, turning slowly. "I don't understand."

"I know you don't, boy. That's why I'm not going to blame you for whatever comes with the dawn."

His grandfather walked back toward the house. At the fire pit, his mind wandered as he watched the night sky. At some point, Darby put her arm around Rand's waist. "Come with me," she said.

They hopped in her pickup truck. She backed out of the endless gravel drive like she'd been driving since she was knee-high to a grasshopper. It'd been sometime before midnight when he'd upped the dose on Grandma's morphine. Hours after midnight when his flashlight beam hit the tombstones. The digital clock on the dashboard showed it was coming up on four in the morning.

"You remember what I told you? About how the females find the weakest twigs? Slice them open, and lay their eggs?"

Rand muffled an acknowledgment, thoughts of the last few hours too heavy on his mind to want to engage in conversation.

"The queen will come with the dawn. Only the species your grandpa was talking about, the queen needs more than the fluid of dying plant-life to satiate her appetite. Rand, I'm sorry. But your grandma was the weakest twig."

Those words took a moment to register. But when they did, he turned to her.

"What the hell are you talking about?"

They'd pulled into a horseshoe-paved driveway. She hopped out of the truck and slammed her door. Rand followed her. They walked up to a slanted twister door, tilted from the ground up toward the house. She swung it open, revealing a steep stone staircase. Darby flipped a switch, and a single bulb illuminated the dirt floor of the cellar. They descended.

Along the back wall was a cork bulletin board. Pushpins with little numbers written on tags taped to them littered the board. Most were white, a few were pink. One was red.

"What is this?" he asked.

"My dad keeps this chart. As the county doctor, he knows who's closest to dying. Who's the weakest twig." She pulled the red pin from the board and handed it to him. "Your grandmother. She could've gone to hospice but refused. She knew she was going to die, and she didn't want anyone else to take her place. If she just could've made it to the dawn, we'd all be safe for another seventeen years."

Rand took the pin that Darby handed him. Then he looked at the board.

"So, you're trying to tell me, some uber-cicada comes out of the ground, and kills one of us every seventeen years? And the sickest on the block just lines up for the slaughter?"

"Something like that," Darby said.

"And if I'd let Grandma live, this queen bee—"

"Queen cicada."

"—would've slit her open, laid its eggs in her, and drunk her body fluids for nourishment. And you would all just sit around and let it happen?"

Darby took his hand and led him to a wooden door with a padlock. She used a key from a chain around her neck to unlock it. Standing under the bright light, he noticed a butterfly-shaped rash over the bridge of her nose and across her cheeks.

"You've got a rash on your face," he said.

"Dad says it's just a heat rash. Too much time in the sun," she said.

When the door swung open, Rand saw a glowing light from across the far wall, even though Darby hadn't touched anything. As he inched closer, he saw a giant bug-shaped shell, nearly as tall as he was. *The wings*. The veined wings sparkled as though they'd been dipped in gold, and rolled in diamonds, bioluminescent from some inner glow. They were mesmerizing. In the swirling details of the veined wings were symbols. Letters and words. As he looked closer, Rand's brain took the image and began forming words in his mind.

Submit the weakest of your kind,
To our demand do not be blind.
Choose to deny us,
Man's demise will be found,
When riseth the beast
'Neath Fallow Ground.

"Who made these?" Rand asked, not able to draw his gaze away from the glittering wings.

"My great-great-grandfather found this exoskeleton, and put it here. You see the message, too? When you glance at it, or look from the corner of your eye, it's gibberish. Intelligent symbols, but indecipherable. But straight on, the shapes swim around until they form words we can understand. Dad thinks even the French traders and Native Americans understood them. We don't have a choice but to sacrifice one person every seventeen years. If we don't, they'll rise and destroy us all."

"And now that Grandma's gone, who will it be?" he asked.

Darby walked over to the bulletin board. There were a few pink pushpins. She pulled the one with a number two taped to it.

"When you went for your walk with your grandpa, Dad told me. It's Jessica Hyde. We're picking her up on our way back. She's only fifteen. She had cancer when she was younger, but I'd thought she was in full remission. Until tonight."

Rand pulled open a file cabinet and started flipping through it. He pulled out file number one. Grandma. He read the reports from the last few years as her health declined. He shoved the file back in the cabinet and pulled out number two. His eyes roamed over the diagnostic sheet. Lupus. Chronic. Symptoms included fatigue, bruising easily, and a butterfly rash across the face. He flipped to the first page and saw the name at the top of the chart.

"Darby," he whispered. She looked over at him.

"What is it?"

"Jessica Hyde isn't number two." Numb, he dropped the file into her hands, then realized what he'd blurted out. He held her as she read it. Supported her as her knees went weak, and wiped the tears from her cheeks as she wept. It didn't matter that she might have another ten years. That was ten years less than the next sickest person around.

They got back in her truck. Rand drove. They were both silent for several minutes, until Darby spoke.

"You know why your grandmother was deaf in one ear?" she asked, her voice sounding hollow.

"No," Rand said, keeping his eyes on the road. A faint glow shone on the eastern horizon.

"When you were a year old, you got meningitis. Your pin moved to number one. Just before the dawn, your mom swallowed some pills and didn't tell anyone until it was too late to save her. Your grandpa and my dad stayed by your crib, seeing you through the fever. Your grandma stayed by her daughter's side, out in the center of the fallow ground. She put one hand over her left ear and kept it there when the beast erupted. Held it there while the creature sang its mating song, which must've been ear-piercing, and while it slit your mother open to lay its eggs."

Rand wanted to squeeze his eyes shut to block out the image. "Why didn't she just cover both ears?" he asked, suspecting the answer.

"Because she wouldn't let go of your mother's hand."

When they reached Grandpa's farm, Rand helped Darby out of the cab of the truck, and they made their way to the center of the dead field. His grandfather and Doc Swanson were waiting.

"Where's Jessica?" the doc asked. "I thought you were going to pick her up."

Darby shook her head. "Dad, Jessica's going to live to a ripe old age."

The ground trembled, and the doc screamed. "No, I might've been wrong. You could have longer to live."

"Dad, it's OK," Darby said, as she lay down, her hair blending in with the dried golden grass. "It's in the county covenants. Any of us who stay here past the age of thirteen knows what we're risking. If I'm going to die young anyway, I'd rather it just take me, and not the whole world." Her dad was shaking and crying so hard he couldn't form words. The doc limped away, collapsing beyond the graveyard. Darby looked to Rand. He wondered if she still found the cicadas romantic. She must've read his mind.

"Wish this weren't my role. But it's still pretty amazing, right?" Her voice sounded thick. She was choking back tears. "I mean, they survive seventeen years down there. That's my whole life. Then they struggle to get here, just to reproduce." Her sky-blue eyes blinked.

"Will it hurt?" she asked.

"I don't know. If it does, you just squeeze my hand."

The land trembled for miles around them. Without thinking, Rand raised her, bringing her lips to his. He kissed her like this was her first kiss, and his last. It was rushed, desperate, and deep. The ground burst open and insect-like legs clawed their way to the surface. Darby pulled away, and they both turned toward the beast. The thing was terrifying and beautiful at the same time. It lumbered to the Black Gum tree, and leaning against it, began to molt. The back split down the middle, and a pulsing, white fleshy beast climbed out of the shell. Within seconds, its surface took on a glossy, golden sheen. Wings shook forth, drying in the morning wind and glinting in the first rays of daylight. Millions of smaller creatures burst forth from the field and a deafening symphony began. Rand held Darby's hand and cupped his other hand over one ear.

After mating, the queen circled Darby like a dog sniffing its meal. It found the weakest parts of her and slit her open.

Her scream pierced the dawn and carried across the fallow land. Her hand clenched Rand's so tightly, he eventually lost all feeling in that arm.

Darby's breaths were shallow when the nymphs broke free of their eggs deep inside her. Rand saw her skin begin to move, and couldn't turn his eyes away as her belly tore open. Hundreds of the creatures fled from their womb and used their powerful front legs to dig. They disappeared, burrowing deep beneath the dying field.

Rand heard only silence, until he turned. Then he could've sworn he made out the faint voice of his grandmother calling him from beneath the Black Gum tree to come in for breakfast.

After they'd buried Darby in the graveyard, Rand looked out over the land. His grandfather had explained to him, over the generations, man had tried every weapon invented to kill the queen. They were impervious to fire and ice. To bullets and blades. Chemical sprays couldn't permeate that shell. So there had always been a sacrifice. But Rand thought about those few seconds, right after she molted. Before the shell grew golden and hard. When she was still a fleshy, pulsing vulnerable newborn.

And he knew, seventeen years from now, he'd be right here waiting for her.

ADVERSE POSSESSION

Willard pulled his hat farther down over his ears as a whir of snowflakes swirled around his face, biting his cheeks.

Between coughs, Tommy was droning on about the land, pointing out the various headstones and whom they belonged to. You'd think the guy was making introductions at a dinner party. Willard looked past his old poker buddy and saw the glow of the fading fire through the window in the house up the hill.

"Now the Burtons here," Tommy said, "they were the ones who put the reinforcements in the bridge that crosses the crick. God bless'm for that." The wind picked up even more, howling through the trees. From behind them, in the direction of the denser woods, Willard heard the cracking of brittle limbs and the sudden shriek of an animal. The sound cut off almost as soon as it had begun, but Tommy snapped to attention, frozen for a moment, only his eyes moving as they searched the forest. He choked out another cough, then moved in the direction of the house.

Finally.

They stepped onto the bridge and Tommy pointed out some rotted planks.

"Meant to fix those last spring. The planks're in the shed." He looked around again, his eyes lost and haunted. Willard thought Tommy might actually be considering going to get the planks and fixing the bridge right now. Below them, the water's surface was frozen, decaying leaves trapped in its icy grip. Beneath the brittle surface, something dark flowed back and forth.

"I'll take care of it, Tommy. You're leaving her in good hands." *Numb hands at this point.*

Tommy nodded. He towered over Willard and weighed at least twice as much, but once they'd stepped off the bridge on the other side, he seemed to deflate a little.

They walked up the hill toward the house. With his large, gloved hands, Tommy grabbed a couple of logs from a snow-dusted wood pile. He nudged the door open with his boot and went straight to the hearth. The fire had mostly died down, and when he tossed the first log in, weak flames licked at it from the ashes.

Willard moved toward the stove—*my stove as soon as the papers are signed*—and put on a kettle. He pulled two blue-speckled mugs from a cupboard and set them on the kitchen table.

As the fire cracked and sputtered, Tommy pulled off his gloves and hat and unbuttoned his coat, sending a shower of snowflakes onto the linoleum floor. What was left of Tommy's white hair looked matted to his head in some places, sticking out wildly in others. Willard scooped some instant coffee into the mugs, already having decided a real coffee pot would be one of the first additions to his new home.

Tommy pulled open a desk drawer and grabbed some pens. The paperwork was already on the kitchen table, being guarded by a ceramic rooster and a wide-eyed, owl-faced napkin holder.

The kettle whistled, its shrill cry cutting through the otherwise silent house. Willard filled the cups, watching the steam rise. Both men took a seat at the table.

"Well," Tommy said, "I guess this is it. Most folks don't want to buy land that includes a cemetery, even though I dropped the price to rock bottom. The thought of it scares most, and the duty to maintain the easement scares off the rest." He took a sip of his coffee. His words were slow, deliberate. He looked Willard in the eye. "You do understand, that's part of the sale. You buy the property, you must maintain the easement."

Willard shifted in his seat. "Well, sure, Tommy. But you said no one's visited that graveyard in over thirty years. How hard can it be?"

Tommy's jaw clenched. "It don't matter. Whatever, whoever

needs access to or from, you gotta respect that. You won't just own this land now. You're responsible for it. And for everything on it." He'd worked himself up and fell into a coughing fit. He pounded one fist into his chest a few times. Willard moved to get out of his chair to assist, but Tommy scowled and waved him back down.

Tommy reached for a pen and scribbled his name, Thomas Fitting, on the land sale form. Willard reached across the table, pulling paper and pen closer. He signed it as well, Willard Cowell.

"I'll leave you to it then," Tommy said. He slipped back into his coat, clomped across the linoleum floor, and took his key ring from a hook near the door. "One last thing, in the cellar, there's a—" He looked out the window, in the direction of the graveyard. Distracted, he repeated, "There's a—," then he got a queer look on his face, strange enough that Willard followed his gaze to see what had caught his attention. A swirl of snow, darkened by dirt, skirted the far side of the creek. Willard heard a loud thump and turned back to see Tommy lying supine on the floor, his face a twisted grimace.

"Tommy?" he said, dropping to his knees. Willard gripped his hand, and for a moment he was certain his fingers were about to snap under the pressure. Tommy's now-bluish lips moved, but only a wheezing sound escaped as his eyes glazed over.

Willard stood, grateful that the old bastard's ticker had held on long enough for them to complete the sale. He used the old pea-green wall phone, its cord twisted and tangled, to make a pointless call to 911. He sipped his coffee, letting the warmth of it move down his throat as he watched the dark cloud of snow dancing along his creek.

Willard woke up on the couch to the sound of animals screeching in flight. Over the past month, he'd grown accustomed to the black silhouettes of bear and moose sewn into the cushions. To the stuffed trout hanging on the wall. He'd even gotten used to the shadows that seemed to pass outside his window at night. But he still couldn't abide that brief yet piercing bestial screeching.

Blinding mid-morning sunlight now shone on the large icicles hanging from the eave. He listened to the *drip drip drip* as the drops fell into the slush beneath the window. He swung open the lock on the sill and tried to lift the window. At first it didn't budge, but then the winter-long seal released, and he slid the window up. The fresh breeze he'd anticipated was quickly overpowered by something else. The word *carcass* came to mind. Something had died out there. Willard slammed the window shut, causing an icicle to plunge and shatter. He went to the kitchen and made scrambled eggs for breakfast. Halfway through, fork midway to his lips, he caught himself staring at the portion of the floor where Tommy had taken his last breath.

About an hour later, he slid on his boots and coat and headed out the back door. He saw the axe leaning against the woodpile, and thought again of Tommy, who'd probably chopped all of this himself.

As Willard walked down the hill, the smell of death grew even stronger. He was almost across the bridge when he heard a wet splintering sound, and his foot shot out from under him. He flung his hands out to his sides to grab the railing, and looked at the hole he'd just made in the rotten plank. He took a wide step over the missing area, noticing the dark swirling in the water below. *Friggin' Tommy.* He coulda had the decency to fix that damn thing before he kicked it.

Willard moved through the graveyard.

"Mrs. Pritchard, you're looking lovely today," he said. "Don't suppose you'd be so kind as to point me in the direction of the dead body?" He hadn't really paid much attention to these stones during Tommy's tour, but he looked closer now. Eleanor Pritchard. Beloved Wife Mother, 1748–1810. Steward 1810–

A winged skull was etched into the stone. Its empty round eyes reminded him of the owl that still sat on his kitchen table. He looked at the next headstone. Jonathon Pritchard. Faithful Husband Father, 1739–1814. Steward 1814–

An identical winged skull was also at the top center of his stone. He continued looking at the other graves. Other families. All had a name, year of birth and death. Although the design of the winged skull varied slightly over the years, the image appeared on every stone. And all had that curious "Steward" designation, with a year and a dash beside it. Willard shook his head and went back to looking for the source of the putrid stench.

As he moved deeper into the woods, he was surprised to still see the occasional grave. Some were just a flat stone slab, the words so worn away he couldn't make them out. Then he came to a mound. *Surely not,* he thought. *A burial mound?*

He felt a crunching under his boots, and scuffed at the melting snow. At first, Willard thought it was just a tree branch. He knelt, and lifted it in his bare hand. He ran one finger up and down the slender curve and recognized it for what it was.

A bone.

He got up and walked around the mound, and saw a pyramidal structure made of weathered stone slabs. He guessed the base to be six by six. His gaze moved up the steps of the altar, where more bones, jaws, teeth, and antlers lay scattered. But it was seeing what was draped *across* the altar that caused a cold spike to race down his spine. A coyote carcass, tongue hung slack, one eye glazed over, the other missing. The same sunlight that had started the slow process of melting his icicles had begun its work here, too. A gaping hole in the animal's side revealed ribs and flesh. But not enough flesh. *Something's been feeding.* And were those claw marks ripped into the stone?

Willard looked around and realized that there were hundreds of animal bones, but no tracks. In fact, he couldn't remember seeing any animals, or tracks, anywhere on the property. Searching the ground, all he could make out were long drag marks in the melting snow and in the dirt. He remembered the look on Tommy's face when he'd heard that animal shrieking from the depths of the forest. That animal's death cry had put Tommy on guard. But against what? Willard's heart started pounding, and he broke for the house then, racing through the woods, around the headstones. Out of breath, he paused, gripping a stone for support. He was trembling, or at least thought he was. A knot began to form in the pit of his stomach when he realized it was the stone that was vibrating.

"What the—?"

He stepped back. Same winged skull. Thomas Fitting. 1935–2013. Steward 2013–

"Tommy?" Willard asked. His voice cracked as he said it, and he realized he was on the verge of hysterics. Now he *was* trembling. He reached out toward the stone, sunlight glinting off something in it that sparkled. The moment he touched it, he felt the vibration and jumped back as though he'd been bitten.

"No, no you did not!"

Willard raced across the bridge and scrambled up the hill. He slipped and began sliding down toward the creek. He clawed at the ground, gripping roots until his descent was halted. Lying on his side, panting, he focused on his task.

Calm the fuck down.

He slowed his breathing, then stood and made his way up the hill. Cold mud soaked through the knees of his jeans from when he'd fallen, and he shivered.

He walked into the house, oblivious to the mud he was tracking in. *Screw it. It's not my house. Not my floor. It's Tommy's. And the Burton's. And the Pritchard's. And whoever the hell was buried in that mound.* He felt a rage welling inside him. He stormed toward the table, grabbed the ceramic rooster by the neck, and hurled it at the wall. It shattered, and its head bounced back toward him, coming to rest at his feet. He kicked it and it skittered away, disappearing around the corner. Willard looked toward the owl napkin holder.

"You're next." But he went straight to the fridge and grabbed a can of beer. He gulped half of it before approaching the kitchen window. Tommy's window. He stood back a little, wanting to see out, but not wanting to be seen. He slugged down the rest of the brew. He grabbed what was left of the six pack by its plastic ring and pulled a chair up to the window, little white, red and black shards of rooster peppering the floor around him. As he drank, Tommy's words came back to him.

"*You must maintain the easement. Whatever, whoever needs access to or from, you gotta respect that. You won't just own this land now. You're responsible for it. And for everything on it.*"

Willard finished his fourth beer, and then shuffled through

the desk, ransacking papers and slamming drawers until he found what he wanted. The deed to the house.

He scanned it, his vision a bit blurry. Taxes *blah blah.* Easement to the cemetery. Adverse Possession Clause. *Failure of the landowner to defend his property may result in the property permanently reverting to a previous dweller.*

The windows were shut, but Willard could swear the stench of that rotting coyote had found its way into the house. What else had Tommy been trying to tell him? He plopped down onto a kitchen chair and started in on another beer. When he began to doze off, the can slipped from his hand, dropping to the floor and toppling over. Beer began to gurgle and stream out of the opening. Willard watched as little piss-colored streams carried bits of shattered rooster across the floor.

The cellar.

It was the last thing Tommy was talking about, right before he dropped. Willard had thought about going down there. Tried a few times. But the steps seemed too steep, too narrow. Nothing down there was worth twisting his knee. And, truth be told, whenever he stood there at the top of those stairs, he remembered that look on Tommy's face when he mentioned the cellar, and that was enough to give him pause. Now, Willard stood and walked across the hardwood floor of the family room. He stumbled, knocking the stuffed trout on the wall askew. He moved to the back hallway and stood in front of a doorway. Layers of paint peeled from its surface. Eggshell white, and underneath that, robin's egg blue.

Willard swayed a little, but reached for the dark handle and opened the door. He made his way down the steps, his knees and the warped wood beneath him creaking with each step. The walls were old cement block. He stood in a single shaft of light shining from the hallway above. He moved his arm around until he felt a chain, and pulled. The room was illuminated by a single bulb suspended from the ceiling. The cellar had a dirt floor. A pile of arrowheads and a crumpled, rusty musket lay discarded in one corner. An unfinished brick wall jutted out from the south side of the room. He moved around it and saw a stone leaning against the brick. *But not just a stone,* his mind insisted. A *tomb*stone. The side facing him was blank. He had to know.

Willard leaned down, the effects of the beer causing his head to swim. He put his hands on the headstone and tugged until it leaned away from the wall. The bulb above him was swinging in a dizzy frenzy, causing the letters and the shadows from the etching to stretch and shrink.

Willard Cowell.

Upon seeing his own name, he snatched his hands away from the stone. It dropped toward him, scraping along the front of his shin and smashing his foot. Willard howled, and yanked his leg until his foot was free. Blood began to seep through his jeans, along the area where his shin now burned.

He'd only seen it for a moment, but it was definitely his name etched into the headstone. And that same, haunting winged skull. Had Tommy done that?

He lurched up the stairs and made his way through the house to the back door. He stood in the open doorway, breathing deeply. Squinting, he looked across the creek, beyond the graves. He couldn't see the altar, but he knew it was there. And whatever had been feeding on that wild dog was there, too.

Tommy had been trying to tell him something. To explain. About the stewards. He was so damned insistent about maintaining the bridge. So that whoever, *whatever* needed access could pass. How long had that been going on here? From the looks of the cemetery, and the burial mound, hundreds of years at least. But Willard didn't sign up for that. He just wanted some cheap land and privacy. The land this side of the creek would have to do. Not only was he not going to repair the bridge. He now planned to destroy it.

The axe, dull and silent, beckoned him. He grabbed it and limped down the hill toward the creek. He slipped and went down on his injured leg. When he stood again, blood stained the snow. Willard took a tenuous step up to the bridge. He thought of the parade of shadows he'd seen outside his window. The screeching of the animals in flight. The claw marks scratched into the altar.

Why hadn't the others thought of this? Half-drunk and

half-crazed, he laughed at his own ingeniousness. Giddy, he swung the axe high and felt the jolt run up his arm as the axe bit into the wood. He swung again. And again. The sun was setting, hiding behind the trees. Something dark swirled in the water below him. As he made more progress, the thing's movements became more frantic.

"Good, you son of a bitch. Without the bridge, you can't come up my way anymore, can you?" Willard cackled and kicked out a plank. His foot went through the hole, and he could swear that blackness swirled and raised up with the water, hungry, reaching for him, just before he pulled his leg back up.

Panting, he looked to the graveyard. The shadows of the headstones grew long in the sunset. Then they began to move.

"No," he whispered. He could taste stale beer on his breath, and a hint of bile made its way up his throat. His head was pounding. Willard looked to the water and screamed. "No!"

He swung the axe in a fury now. He heard moaning coming from across the creek. He heard the wood splinter under the force of his blows. He glanced up to see the shadows moving toward him. He realized with a deafening certainty that these were the shadows that passed outside his window each night. Tears were pooling in his eyes and spilling down his cheeks. His entire body was shaking. At last he chopped through the last remaining log holding the bridge up. It collapsed into the creek. A wave of elation swept over him as he cried and laughed at the same time.

"Ha, take that!"

One of the shadows approached the far side of the creek bed. It was moaning. But then it said a word. It said his name.

"W..i..l..l..a..r..d..."

Somehow, he knew it was Tommy.

"You shoulda warned me, Tommy. You did me wrong."

The apparition moved closer, groaning, clearing its throat until he could understand it. It sounded gravelly as it spoke. Every word was an effort.

"The animals know this is a hunting ground. They flee until we herd them here. The bridge lets us pass, so we can seek its nourishment. We can't cross over water. Without the bridge, we are trapped here. But *it* is not. And without a feeding, it grows hungry." The Tommy-Thing sounded forlorn with its next words. "It will be hunting soon."

The darkness rose out of the water. Willard stumbled backward and slammed into the ground. The inky liquid licked the ground, his boot, the blood from his shin, like a tongue. The decayed leaves, the earth itself, drew forward, a chaotic, ravenous mass. Willard flipped to his stomach and clawed his way up the hill. A growl echoed behind him just before something sharp raked his back. He screamed, but a huge earthy claw clamped down across his mouth, muffling his shrieks. He instantly understood, as horrifying as the animal screams were, why they never lasted long. The axe lay nearby and he swiped for it, but another claw gripped his ankle and began dragging him down the hill. The icy water chilled him as he was sloshed through the creek. His lungs were burning as he tried to scream, but still the beast pressed down on his mouth. At one point his head struck a rock, and he blacked out from the pain.

When he awoke, he saw the starlit sky above him. He tried to sit up, but found that his wrists and ankles were bound. His eyes opened wide as he swung his head back and forth, frantic. Roots. Roots held him fast. He was on the altar, but something seemed different. Something was missing.

The burial mound.

He heard a sniffing and sensed something behind him. Then he realized where the mound had gone. It was circling him, that dark tongue licking his cheek, moving down his neck. It went lower and he stiffened. It moved past his waist to his leg. It slid up and down his shin, salivating over the taste of his blood. Then the mouth of the beast opened further, revealing rows and rows of teeth, just before they sank into his flesh and ripped out a chunk of his leg. The graveyard shadows stood back, silent witnesses to the slaughter.

Willard thrashed against the agonizing torrents of pain that unrelentingly racked his body. The roots, sprouting thorns, tightened, digging into his wrists and ankles. He tried to scream, but a new tendril snaked and constricted around his throat, rendering him utterly helpless. He squeezed his eyes shut, but opened them when he felt a familiar hand grip his. Tommy.

Out of the tear-blurred corner of his eye, Willard could see what remained of the coyote. Every bone was picked clean. He thought of his headstone and knew it wouldn't stay in the cellar much longer. He hoped he'd make a better steward than he had a landowner. And as he squeezed Tommy's hand in a death grip, he hoped the coyote hadn't suffered long.

THE FIRE TOWER

Lorne pulled the trail map from his pocket. It took him the better part of a week to find it. After digging through drawers and searching through closets, he finally found it in an old box of photographs in the garage. The map was faded and coffee-stained, but as he read it, some of the landmarks sparked clear memories. The cave, the old swimming pool, the nature center. Others sparked images from the photographs he'd leafed through. The falls and the overlook. One that was clear in his mind was the fire tower.

Now that he was in the park, it seemed funny looking at the key for the trails. A thick line for a paved road. A thin line for moderate trails. A broken line, a series of dashes, for a rugged trail. The scent of scorched forest had been strong for hours. Every trail was rugged now. Off limits.

He and Debra left their jeep outside of the park entrance. They walked past the unmanned guard shack and climbed over a drooping chain.

Soot and ashen remains scattered the forest floor. But even so, life was struggling to take hold again. Dark shoots pierced the ground, reaching skyward. Some kind of pollen floated in the air, small white tufts carried on the breeze. A few had caught in Debra's dark hair. It gave Lorne a glimpse of what she might look like as she began to gray, and he wondered if they'd grow old together. Nettles clung to her socks and shorts.

Lorne told her about coming here as a kid with his grandparents. Grandpap manned the fire tower from 1952 until they decommissioned it sometime in the '70s. By the time they spent summer holidays here, it had been opened for the park visitors to climb the 120 metal steps. The lookout tower, what Grandpap called the "cab," was over a hundred feet in the air. That view used to look out over thousands of trees. What was left now were just dark splinters against the sky.

When he'd walked these trails as a kid, Grandpap always warned Lorne to stick to the path or he'd risk getting poison ivy or poison oak. He could always hear something rustling off in the brush and they'd make guesses about what it might be. Squirrel, rabbit, wood mice. There shouldn't be anything living out there now, but Lorne could swear he heard something rustling through the ashes, snaking its way through the soot.

When they came to the base of the tower, they saw the sign, toppled over. To Debra, it must've looked like any piece of debris. Lorne could see some teeth marks, like something had been chewing on it. And he could make out random letters. He remembered a photo. Smiling, somewhat toothless as a kid. He remembered what the sign had said. "Throwing objects off the tower is strictly prohibited."

Debra peeked over his shoulder. "So, you want to take the butterfly trail or climb the Fire Tower? Either way we'll still make it back to the inn in time to join the shuffleboard tournament."

She was joking of course. Lorne had seen the images on the news and knew what had become of the inn. The sheriff had described it as a tinder box. They never did find Grandpap's body. A newlywed couple who checked out early that morning said they saw him on the overlook behind the dining room after breakfast. Said he was drinking coffee and watching the songbirds feed. A family headed to the saddle barn swore they saw him on the Butterfly Trail. Fortunately for the family and the horses, the fire didn't reach as far as the stables. Lorne's mind replayed those images from the news, the body-shaped ash clumps in the racquetball courts, on the lounge chairs around the pool, in the rocking chairs on the west patio. No one would be playing shuffleboard tonight.

Lorne let out something less than a chuckle. "The view's really great from up there."

They had talked about the safety of climbing it. The tower and the steps were made of steel. The forest fire did a lot of damage, but climbing shouldn't pose a hazard. He paused, hesitant. "Ladies first?"

"As much as I appreciate your chivalry, I'll let you take the lead on this one."

Lorne climbed the first short flight of steps. They were steep, and went in a zig zag pattern. Nine steps up in one direction. About face. Nine steps up again. Repeat.

About halfway up, he paused. Not out of breath, just thinking about what they were doing. He had been on these steps so many times with his grandfather. He looked down at that toppled warning. Vines wound around the steel beams. Black thistles clung to Debra's pants. Something glinted in the distance. He squinted. Something flashed in an erratic pattern and then stopped. He felt lightheaded.

They kept climbing and made it to the underside of the cab. Whatever lock used to hold it closed had long since vanished. The cab, a little one room lookout, had been mostly made of wood and glass. Lorne wondered whether it survived the fire. The underside of the deck looked singed. He pushed on the trapdoor and it swung upwards. A puff of ashes fell down on him, and settled in his lungs.

He looked down at Debra, a pale ray of hope against a burnt out landscape. He took a step upward and hefted himself into the cab.

The floorboards showed no signs of the fire from the inside. The room was as he'd remembered. Ten by ten, knee-high bead board, then windows all around. He silently held one hand out toward Debra, indicating she should wait until he'd tested it. As he walked around the room, the boards creaked, but held. He waved her up.

Once she had joined him, Debra looked around, taking in the view.

"Wow," she whispered.

Lorne noted the items in the room. A telescope lay haphazardly in the corner. A pair of work boots was neatly placed along the wall.

Lorne glanced around and looked across the burnt landscape. Twenty, maybe twenty-five miles in each direction. The ruined blackness was in the inner circle of his view, but beyond that was green. The fire hadn't done near the damage it had intended to.

But the green didn't look right. It didn't look...*normal*.

Debra was pulling the burrs from her clothing. She winced in pain.

"You ok?" Lorne asked.

She grinned and held her thumb out toward him. "Little fucker bit me." She tugged on the splinter and pulled most of it out. Lorne inspected her thumb and saw a dark remnant deep in her flesh. A dot of blood pooled.

A sudden *thunk* from above startled him and Debra let out a yell. They both breathed heavily.

"A bird?" she asked.

He shook his head. *I don't know.*

He looked upward, toward the source of the sound. He'd remembered the cab roof as solid, but now he noticed another trap door above them.

"What the—"

He reached up and his fingertips brushed the wood.

He joined his hands and hoisted Debra up. She pushed on the door and it swung away. He lifted her higher. She climbed up and then dropped a rope ladder to him.

Lorne climbed it and within seconds was by her side on the roof of the cab. Another set of steep zigzag steps ascended above them.

"That can't be right. I've never seen this."

"Maybe you just can't see it from the ground. Or your grandfather didn't want you climbing this high."

Maybe.

As they climbed, Lorne felt the tower swaying slightly in the breeze. If it hadn't fallen in all these years, it wasn't going to fall today. Still, he felt the sensation of vertigo. The ground seemed to swim. The burnt out circle became smaller. It was an optical illusion, but the rest of the forest looked wrong. Rays of sunlight tried to hit the leaves, but twisted and left patches of blackness that should've been light. He remembered how a western breeze used to make the leaves of the forest look like they'd been brushed by a gentle wave. A flutter would swell, smaller branches would bend in unison, toward the east. But now, things moved in an unnatural way. Black, skeletal limbs bent toward the tower, then released, momentarily escaping. It was as though the tower inhaled, drawing the remnants of the forest near. Upon the hint of an exhale, the cremated woods drooped outward, but didn't escape. For a panicked moment, Lorne felt the oxygen from his lungs being sucked away, and realized even the air around him moved in a way that seemed alive.

Debra came up behind him, and it struck him that her footfalls seemed unnatural. Before, there had been a human rhythm to them. Now, they were disjointed, foreign. Lorne turned back to look at her. There were hundreds of those brambles clinging to her clothes. How could that be happening when they weren't on the trail anymore? She'd had her head down, watching her footing, but when she sensed that he had stopped, she raised her face to him. Dark spiny spikes were poking out of her cheek. As he watched, a cluster began to break through her lower lip. She didn't even seem to notice. Just grinned and said, "Some view, huh?" Her words sounded garbled and Lorne tried to convince himself those things were not the new surface of her tongue. There wasn't room to move past her without risking those things pricking him. He turned away from her and kept climbing.

They got to the next level, and it wasn't a cab, just a platform. "What is that?" Debra asked.

Lorne didn't know. It was some kind of mirror on a swivel. He moved it and flicked a shutter. In the distance, something answered back. Flicks of light, in rapid succession. Debra looked in the mirror, horror spread across her face. She put one hand over her left eye, and ran her fingers along her face, almost as though making sure it was still there. Lorne felt puzzled.

"Oh my God, don't you see it?" she screamed at him.

They had to be two hundred feet up by now, but it felt like more. Debra grabbed the mirror and the shutter. She began signaling to the light in the distance. It flickered again and she doubled over as though she'd been punched. She wretched a few times, and vomited over the side of the platform.

"Throwing objects off the tower is strictly prohibited," Lorne said casually.

"Does breakfast count?" she asked, seeming genuinely concerned about whether or not she'd broken a rule.

Something flew by. It had the helicopter movements of a hummingbird or a dragonfly. But there was a clicking sound. A scent carried on the wind, not the burnt smell that had invaded Lorne's throat and lungs all morning, but the smell of decay. The odor of things long dead.

Debra raised herself up. She began to flick the shutter again. Slowly at first, but then so rapidly, she couldn't keep up with whatever was answering back. A pair of glasses, or spectacles as Grandpap had always called them, lay broken and twisted on the platform.

Lorne thought back to that last summer Grandpap brought him here. How they'd climbed to the cab, and Lorne stood on his tip toes to look out the open window. Even at a hundred twenty feet, those extra few inches might've made all the difference in his view. Grandpap had stared off to the east, up at the low hung clouds. He took off his spectacles and cleaned them with his flannel shirt. He rubbed his eyes.

"Something wrong?" Lorne asked.

"*Just the damn floaters.*" *Grandpap had always described the floaters in his eyes as seeing strings, or cobwebs, across his field of vision.*

"Bad cobwebs today?"

"*Cobwebs that've caught a bunch of dark shapes, squirming and squiggling in their trap.*" *He started it as a tease, or at least Lorne thought he had, but then a look of concern spread over the old man's face.* "Do you see those flashes?" *He pointed over the forest floor and then gestured up toward the clouds. Lorne looked and looked but couldn't see. There was irritation in the old voice now.* "Those silver lights, dancing and hiding, all over the sky."

He'd asked his Grandpap to lift him up. He felt those old warm, wrinkled hands grip him around the waist and set him in the window ledge. "Higher!" *he squealed. He wanted to see the lights, too, and wished he had floaters in his eyes. Grandpap was holding him out over the edge and Lorne felt giggly.*

"Can I toss my gum wrapper over the edge?"

Grandpap hesitated, confused. "I don't know. Can you?"

"Well, the sign said no throwing objects off the tower."

"Are you sure?" *He looked suspicious.*

"Silly, we've read it a hundred times."

Grandpap looked annoyed, and disappointed. He pulled Lorne back inside the cab and set him down.

Now, as Lorne stood on this dizzying platform, his girlfriend communicating with something on another distant platform, Lorne saw silver flashes darting throughout the sky. When he tried to focus on one, it would disappear. The only way to see them was in his peripheral vision.

He moved a few feet toward Debra. She looked at him. One of those burrs was bursting through her left eye socket. It looked like a spiny black sea urchin, the dark needles like some grotesque mascara fanning up and down. Blood ran down her cheek like red teardrops. He didn't want her signaling to whatever might be out there. He didn't want it to know about him.

Lorne picked her up and cradled her in his arms. He moved toward the edge.

"No throwing objects off the tower," she reminded him.

He kissed her, and those black needles pierced his cheek, tugging as he pulled back.

"I would never objectify you," he said. "You are so much more than a gum wrapper or regurgitated waffles."

A sob caught in her throat, or maybe it was another sea urchin growing there. She whispered a *thank you* as Lorne held her in his outstretched arms. He let go.

For the first few seconds, her plummet was silent. But then the darting, buzzing creatures swarmed at her, and her screams carried up to him. Lorne took the broken spectacles and put them on his face.

He looked up, and saw one final set of steps ascending into the clouds. The air had grown cold and thin. As he climbed, he noticed gray, gooey blobs stuck to the underside of the steps above him. His stomach growled and he was tempted to eat one, but as he reached for it, it turned to dust. The lightheaded feeling he'd experienced earlier persisted. Lorne heard a *tinking* sound from above, and through the slats in the steps he could see a small object bouncing toward him. Somehow it didn't fall or plummet. The gumball hesitated, then rolled toward him. The red orb seemed to blink, and came to a stop on the step at his eye level. He put it in his pocket and climbed until he came upon a little boy. The child was barefoot, and wearing faded overalls. His small hands were covered in ashes. He spit a handful of gumballs from his mouth, and began dropping them onto the steps.

"These kind are better," he said. "No wrappers."

Lorne couldn't find any argument with that.

"I see you found my glasses," the boy said. "Do you see the floaters now?"

Lorne removed the glasses from his face and handed them to the boy. Lorne looked around, and saw the cobwebs dangling from the clouds. The brilliant flashes continued to blink out of the corner of his eye.

"I see them, Grandpap."

The boy popped a gumball in his mouth and began to chew. "They are always there. The lights you can never quite see, the webs you try to ignore until you're trapped in their sticky gooey grip, and by then it's too late." He grimaced and took the gum out of his mouth. He stuck the wad to a step above him, where it joined hundreds of others. "Stale. It's all stale. You think if you put out enough fires in your life, do enough good, it'll make up for the rest. But it doesn't work that way." The boy spit another half a dozen gumballs into his hand. He sighed with disappointment as he studied them, and then dropped an orange one down the steps.

Lorne drummed his fingers on the railing. "I think you left your work boots down in the cab."

"They were big shoes to fill. Too big."

Movement from the clouds caught Lorne's attention, and dozens of lavender-gray tentacles dipped toward him. The boy didn't watch them, he watched Lorne.

Lorne tried to back away as a few of them swung toward him. He lost his balance and slipped. He gripped the railing as his feet flailed in the air. The suction cups on the slimy arms pulsated and those spiny burrs poked out. They slashed at Lorne's hands and arms, but he refused to let go. The creatures that fed on Debra as she fell swarmed underneath Lorne, hungry, and hoping for a meal. But he refused to let go. The tentacles receded into the clouds.

"I'd seen them a few times when I was manning the tower," the boy said. "Convinced myself I was imagining things. Your grandma convinced me I'd had a stroke or something. Maybe hit my head and that explained the strange scratches along my brow. But it was that day I almost tossed you over the edge I knew they were real. This spot is a like a beacon. If I could hide it, burn it down maybe, they couldn't see us and we couldn't see them anymore. Two separate worlds instead of one that doesn't make sense to them or us."

Lorne's hands and arms were straining. He swung one foot and managed to get back to the steps. He gripped his Grandpap around the legs, heaving.

"What do I do?"

"Go back to the platform. Look in the heliograph."

"The what?"

"The mirror, the one with the shutter. Like I said, I thought the fire would break whatever crack lets those things slip through. But it just opened it wider. Here, take these." They boy gave him a handful of gumballs. Red, blue, yellow, orange, white. "They're all rotten except the green ones."

Lorne looked in his palms. "But there isn't any green."

"I know."

Lorne put them in his pocket and went down the steps. He approached the mirror, tilted it toward him. He raised the shutter and in the reflection he saw Debra. The spiny urchin now hung from the end of a violet tentacle that dangled from her eye socket. Her left arm was missing other than a few inches of splintered bone and meat clinging to her shoulder. Much of her flesh was missing, no doubt now in the bellies of the hummingcopters or helibirds. Thistles and burrs covered most of her head and face. Lorne began moving the shutter, and saw images of new-Debra slinking along the Butterfly Trail. New-Debra walking to the truck stop down the highway, leaving her little urchins in the back of every tractor trailer she found, to let them spread throughout the country. He knew these must've been the same images she'd seen. This was why she'd been horrified, and why she thanked him for dropping her from the tower. The clouds were hanging even lower to the ground now, as though they were following him on his descent. The heliograph revealed that everyone could see the floaters now. And the things that lurked in the clouds could reach anyone. The whole world was stale, and there was no more green.

Lorne made his decision and launched himself from the tower. If he did catch up to Debra before she got to the highway, he hoped he'd still try to stop her. But he'd felt the first bites, and already sensed the first spark of transformation. The four-dimensional patterns of the hummingcopters began to feel familiar. Time slowed, and an overwhelming dread seized him in a panic. *How had she been so fearless?* He no longer knew to which world he belonged, only that to save either one, he would have to go into the green. A cloud of pollen whispered to him, pulling the oxygen from his lungs. As he wondered whether he'd help Debra or destroy her, he wasn't sure whether he wanted to survive the fall. Lorne heard the *tinking* of reminders descending from above, and realized those would be awfully big shoes to fill.

CONJURING THE CORPSE CANDLES

"Just more old photos and books. And a few dried up spiders we inherited along with the house," Cole Capron muttered. He heaved a sigh before dropping the lid back down, sending a cloud of dust toward his face. He coughed, and shoved the box away with his foot, leaving a trail in the gritty floor. He glanced toward the small semi-circle window behind his mom. Even through the heavy coating of grime, he guessed it must be near noon.

"Look at this, Cole," his mom said, her grin matching the smiley-face bandana she wore over her salt-and-pepper hair. "It's a whirligig."

"A whirli-what?" he asked, letting his head drop back against the wall, idly studying the cobwebs strung along the roof's crossbeams. "You said I could cut out after lunch. I don't want to spend fall break trapped in this attic."

"The design on this button is so intricate," she said, ignoring him. "Here, look. Hold the loops on the end of the string. That's it. I'll wind the button like this, and…presto!" The button spun in a dizzying frenzy. Cole tried to ignore the cobwebs clinging to the thing, but he felt the vibration in the dark braided string.

Cole's voice was deadpan as the button slowed to a lazy twirl. "Thrilling." He dropped the toy on the box beside him. "What about our BLTs? And hooking up the DVD player?" He swiped a palm across his brow, brushing long black bangs out of his eyes. "Priorities?"

"Fine, I'll take a load downstairs and get the bacon started.

You should really look at this corner where I found the whirligig. There's clay marbles, jacks, all kinds of stuff."

Cole looked toward the corner. Leaning up against the wall was a large iron hoop. Maybe two feet across, a flat two inches wide. His mom must've followed his gaze.

"Ah...that's for playing hoop and stick," she said.

"I didn't ask," he responded, with an air of twelve-year-old annoyance he'd perfected since the divorce.

"It was pretty popular in the 1800s. Very hip among pioneer kids. Your Great-Grandpa Bruns loved it. Or was it Great-great-great...anyway, you push the hoop with a stick and see how far you can make it go before it topples over. Or race it, or crash it into other kids' hoops to see who's the victor."

Cole leaned his head against the wall again, only now he closed his eyes. "I'm sure even in the sticks, Child Protective Services would be concerned about a mom starving her son in a dreary attic."

He heard his mom chuckle, and when he lifted his lids, she was starting down the ladder, crate under one arm, trapdoor held aloft with the other. When her head ducked out of sight, she let go and the door slammed shut with an angry bang. Cole heard a muffled *"Sorry!"*

Cole shook his head. "Hoop and stick." He muttered it with an edge of contempt. He reached over to the braid and button lying limp on the box. "Makes you sound pretty high-tech in comparison," he said, pulling on the loops of the whirligig, watching the dark red button spin. He was walking toward the trapdoor when he heard a *thunk* behind him and turned.

The hoop had slipped away from the wall. And was rolling toward him.

The slamming door must've jarred it from its resting place. It didn't carry the same air of abandonment the rest of the junk up here had. Not *quite* the same layer of dust. Cole's eyes fixed on the hoop, his hands absentmindedly pulling the strings of the whirligig taut, the reddish button a whirling blur in the corner of his eye. The hoop advanced. *Did it just avoid that trunk of old clothing?* And though he saw no other movement in the attic, he could swear he heard a faint dry chattering sound.

He mustn't have been holding tight enough, because suddenly the worn string between his hands snapped away from his fingers. The button went flying, the braid flapping in tow, then skittered across the floor in pursuit of a hiding place under an old chest.

The scent of frying bacon seeped through the floorboards. Cole brushed the cobwebs from his hands and reached out toward the shape rotating toward him.

"Simply make a new wooden one," Grace said over her shoulder, lugging the bucket up the hillside, sloshing water with every step. Her long dark braid swung from side to side like a pendulum. "Papa will not mind if you use a birch from near the pond, so long as you chop the rest for firewood."

"Do not spill so much," Wylie complained, walking a few paces behind his older sister. "Bug Jasper's is iron, and knocks my hoop down every time. He is three years my junior, but still he wins." He shook his head, talking more to the wind than to his sister. "There is nothing I would not give to have a forged-iron hoop."

Grace paused, catching her breath. A thin line of sweat coursing down her back caused her calico dress to cling to her. She untied her bonnet, dipping it in the bucket of stream water, and wrung it out over her face, letting the droplets cascade down her slender neck. With her eyes still closed, face turned toward the setting sunshine, she spoke.

"Wylie Bruns, do you not have more important things to suffer on than whether or not Bug Jasper bests you at a game of hoop and stick?" He remained silent. Grace opened her eyes, and replaced her damp bonnet. "I do not expect Papa is willing to grant you a rim from his wagon wheel, even to best a Jasper. If it is of such import, why do you not call upon the little gremlins of the forest to grant you your wish? What is it the Lenape call them? The Pukwudgie?" Her voice filled with a mocking warbling fearfulness. "The gatekeepers of our darker side." Grace giggled, then hefted her bucket and resumed the trek toward their father's swine barn.

Wylie carried two smaller buckets and prided himself on not having lost a single drop. Nor needing to waste any by cooling his head.

He roamed the dark forest to the east with his gaze and thought about the dozens of times he had called upon the Pukwudgie for that very wish. The times he had waited for the will-o'-the-wisps to appear over Crooked Crump Bog. But the ghost lights never revealed themselves.

They arrived at the side of the barn. Grace lifted the lid off the wooden barrel and poured in the water from her bucket.

"Why do you not call upon them to make you Jeb Jasper's bride?" Wylie retorted. "When we all played games at Gunter's meadow, during Shepherd and Wolf, you allowed him to capture you...over and over. Such a sheep. Two nights running. Even though I could have saved you, within easy reach."

A mischievous smile played across Grace's face as a blush rose to her cheeks.

Wylie dumped the water from one of his buckets into the barrel. "I will tell you why." He had been in the attic the previous night, looking through his Opa's fishing gear. And found a diary tucked in the crook behind the tackle box. Grace had inked her heart's darkest desires there. "Because the two of you are planning to elope."

Grace shoved him in the chest, thick brows furrowing, her chestnut braid swinging over her shoulder. Wylie stumbled backward, sprawling, the water from his second bucket spilling to the ground. Both of them burst into a giddy laughter. Grace's face abruptly darkened as she straightened, and looked out over their father's harvested cornfield. She drew in a hesitant breath.

"What is that?"

Wylie rolled over, then scrambled to his feet. He watched the dancing lights approaching in the twilight. They've come at last. *The wind rustled the trees as he breathed out the answer like a hushed prayer.*

"It's the will-o'-the-wisps."

Cole raced his bike down County Road 600, the chill of the overcast day stinging his face. Even from half a mile away, he could see kids on the basketball court at his new middle school. He rode into the empty parking lot and dropped his bike in the grass. Two girls were using sidewalk chalk to retrace the lines of a faded hopscotch board. A few guys sat around making duck calls with thick blades of grass stretched between cupped hands. Pacing his breaths, Cole approached.

"Anybody want to play hoops?" he asked, unzipping his backpack.

The air suddenly went still. The wiry kid wearing glasses froze. A freckled girl with a mop of strawberry-blond curls dropped her chalk and scootched back. The big blond guy in a letterman's jacket stood up, and took a step toward him.

"That supposed to be funny?" The guy planted himself between Cole and the younger kids.

Cole searched their faces, staring at him like he had a bomb strapped to his chest. He tried to sound casual. "Well, we *are* standing on a basketball court. And I've got a basketball," he said, pulling one from his backpack. He dribbled it a couple times before nesting it between his arm and his side. "Call me crazy but…"

The freckled girl's face went from alarmed to relieved as she exhaled.

"Basketball." She stood and walked up to the larger kid, touching his forearm. "Glenn, he wants to play *basketball*." Her smile grew wider, revealing a gap between her front teeth. There was a collective sigh as the group relaxed. The kid with the glasses even let out a nervous laugh. Glenn looked Cole up and down before relaxing his stance.

"Basketball." He turned toward the group, nodding. "Sure, why not. But a word to the wise," he said, knocking the ball away and sinking a shot into the netless rim before facing Cole again, "We don't use the h-word in Jasper's Corner."

They played three-on-three for a while. Even the strawberry blonde, Maisy, wasn't half bad. After a while, Cole looked at his watch.

"I should get going. Promised my mom I'd meet her at some bonfire we got invited to."

"Lady Jasper's?" Maisy said. "Everyone's going to that. She's our Great-grandmother," she said, gesturing at the skinny kid. "She's ancient. Has *one* good eye and just a few of her own teeth left, and is bent over like a crooked stick. But she makes the best pulled pork sandwiches and cornbread this side of the Ohio."

Maisy was right. Half the town made an appearance at the bonfire. After eating his fill of the best pulled pork this side of the Ohio, Cole finished fourth place in the pumpkin toss, and went on a hayride skirting the edges of Crooked Crump Bog. By the time the few remaining kids were roasting marshmallows and swapping fireside tales, most of the grownups had headed home. A few, including his mom, had gone to a neighbor's down the road to play bridge.

Cole sat around the fire on a split log bench watching Glenn tenderly pull strands of hay from Maisy's curls while she tried not to giggle. Her wiry, glasses-wearing brother, Cleek, offered Cole a steaming mug of mulled apple cider.

Cole allowed the question that had been gnawing at him for hours to bubble to the surface. "So, what was with the weird when I showed up?"

Glenn walked away from Maisy and tossed another log on the fire, sending a shower of sparks skyward. Maisy brushed her golden curls behind her ears. "It's an old county legend," she said. "There's this old game, called..." She paused, and looked at Glenn. The fire cast dancing shadows across their faces. He nodded his ascent, then snapped a twig and chucked it into the flames. "Hoop and stick," she continued. "Kids would push the hoop along—"

"Yeah, I've heard of it." Cole said.

"Anyway, back in the late 1800s, this boy, Wylie Bruns, wanted an iron hoop, and prayed to these little blue-robed woodland spirits, the Pukwudgie. One evening as he and his sister, Grace, were emptying water from the river into a barrel, they saw a group of lights moving toward them across a field. Turns out it was five members of the Jasper clan. Jeb's parents, two uncles, and a cousin. Grace was only fifteen and in love with Jeb, but the Jaspers were wealthy and had other plans for him. They accused Grace of bewitching their eldest. Taunted her about grapevine gossip of her family's notoriety for entrancement. But she remained defiant. They pinned Wylie down while they cut off Grace's hair, and drowned her in the barrel after she refused to break off her engagement."

The light of the bonfire reflected in Cleek's glasses. His voice was hushed as he leaned forward. "Wylie eventually clawed his way free, taking a swath of Jeb's uncle's shirt with him. He came out of the swine barn swinging a mallet, but it was too late. They fled, leaving his lifeless sister in the dust. So he let his anger loose on the barrel, turning the thing to splinters. The water gushed out of it just like her life had gushed out of her. And when the last of the wood had fallen, the forged-iron hoop that had encased the frame of the barrel came rolling toward him."

Cole played the image in his mind. A boy whose dark prayer had been answered. "He got what he wished for."

"He just didn't know what it would cost him," Cleek said. "They say in that moment, he let out a scream that reached the four corners of the county. Startled crows into flight, and chased the last rays of the day into hiding. They say as he held his sister, rocking her with one gentle hand, gripping the hoop so tight in the other he bled into it, even as his tears mixed with the river water spilling from her silent throat, he called upon a dark force of the swamp."

"The Pukwudgie?" Cole asked.

"As the old-timers tell it, what heard his cry that night was the beast that causes even the Pukwudgie to tremble."

Cole looked around at their faces. He could tell Cleek and Maisy had either heard or told the story countless times. It had the rhythm of memorization. What he couldn't discern was whether they believed it or were just trying to spook the new kid. A screen door creaked open and slammed shut. Cole turned to see Lady Jasper approaching.

She inched her way toward them, shawl draped over her shoulders and cane in hand. Glenn went to the porch and retrieved her chair. Her wrinkles were like crevasses in the shadows the fire created. She picked up the story where Cleek had left off, staring into the flames with her one good eye, the quiver of old age in her tone.

"The first to go missing was little Bug Jasper. Only seven years old. Imagine his surprise when he found a perfect hoop while walking home after catching toads at the bog. The last his friends saw, he was spinning it ever faster up Crump Hill. The Jaspers searched high and low. But maybe not low enough. They found signs of a struggle on the bridge that crossed over the bog. Two missing planks, a torn piece of his shirt caught on a bent nail. One of his boots nestled in swamp grass. But they never did find the boy. Drove his mother mad. After all, she'd held that girl's head under the water. She *knew* how cruel a death by drowning was. She wandered aimlessly, wailing for her son."

"You said the first?" Cole asked. The wind rustled through nearby trees, sending down a shower of dried leaves. A tinge of fear crossed Maisy's face.

"Oh, sure," Lady Jasper said. "Squeaky Bo Hollis reported seein' that hoop trundle itself up the hill casting off droplets of water while he was pulling a haywagon down the road. The woman in charge of his rooming house thought he was suffering visions. Put a pity shot of bourbon in the coffee she served alongside his sugar cream pie that night. Before the murder, sometimes boys'd nail pairs of tin squares to their hoops, just to hear the jingly sound they'd make as it rolled. There weren't no squares on Wiley Bruns' hoop when Bug Jasper found it. But Squeaky Bo swore something *was* danglin' from it that evening when it passed him by. Said he could hear the rattle carry to him on the breeze.

"Two years went by. One of Jeb's uncles was at the swamp, clomping past the tadpoles and pondskaters. Was after cattail for his stew. Two young folk out for a stroll thought it was his lantern bobbing, but then the hoop came rolling across the field, and they realized they was seein' will-o'-the-wisps. Or as some call 'em, corpse candles. They heard a scream and a thick splashing. After word got out that he was missing, the girl broke down and told her momma. When they found his body, he was missing a finger. There was a line of frost in the grass, about two inches wide, leading away from the bog. Like whatever'd felled him there was frigid as ice."

Cole recalled the moment he'd reached out to the hoop in his attic. How cold it felt. So cold it nearly burned him. Something rustled in the underbrush near the trees. He shivered and took a long sip of his cider.

"Hoop and stick was the most popular toy in the nation at the turn of the century," Lady Jasper croaked out through what remained of her teeth. A drop of spittle glistened on her lip. "But in Jasper's Corner, it became taboo. The local smithy offered up his forge. Oversaw the hearth as townspeople brought their hoops to the pyre. The children cried of course, the women too for a different reason. As they all looked on, something rose from the inferno. A dark hoop, glowing red hot, rolled away from the heap, leaving a trail of embers in its wake. They say it disappeared, hissing into the bog, leaving the melted corpses of its brethren behind. That cold mangled heap of iron lies there still, just beyond those trees. The rest of the building burned to the ground that very night. Only the charred foundation and hearth remain. All else turned to ash."

Cole recalled the image from the hayride. The exposed and abandoned chimney. The tangled heap of metal…but he hadn't known what it meant.

Maisy fiddled with the fringe on her scarf. She sounded more somber than a thirteen-year-old should. "Dozens of unexplained drownings over a hundred years. Sightings of a hoop that moves by itself. Propels itself even up hill, whispering a skeletal ghost-rattle." The red of her hair seemed even stronger in the glow of the flames.

Glenn had been quiet throughout the telling of the tale, but he looked at Cole, and there was a hint of accusation in his voice. "People say whenever they saw Wylie Bruns' face in that half-circle window in his attic, he'd gone up there to call to the hoop somehow. Because there was always a death."

Cleek readjusted his glasses and added, "And the victim was always missing a finger. They say the bones are sacrificed to the dark entity that powers the monster. And with each death the ghost-rattle grows."

"And ever-esurient," Lady Jasper hissed, "abide the will-o'-the-wisps."

"No one's seen the hoop in over thirty years," Maisy said. She shuddered. "It's no wonder after Wylie died, your mom's uncle moved away and let that house sit empty all this time." Lady Jasper nodded and grunted an agreement.

Cole stood up. "I saw it. This morning. We were going through a bunch of old junk. It—" *rolled toward me. Was so cold.* "It was on the screened-in porch when I left." Leaning against the wall, almost hidden in shadow. "I thought my mom must've brought it down, but—" Expectant looks surrounded him.

"You woke it," Lady Jasper said. Her eye squinted. "Of course, you've got the gift. You carry your father's name, but you're a Bruns through and through." Her words came faster now. "What did you touch to rouse it?" She rose from her chair, anxious, using her cane for support.

"Uh, I don't know," he said, nervous now. She was obviously depending on him for something. "A trunk full of books and papers. Some old clothes, a whirligig, an old rocking chair."

The old woman raised a crooked finger and opened her good eye wide. "Tell me about the whirligig."

"It had an old button on it. Blood-red in color. The design was...an anchor I think. And maybe, a knight's helmet? The string was dark. Braided."

"Of course. Grace had such beautiful dark hair, always in a braid. Wylie would have used her hair for the string. And he got the button when he tore himself from the grip of the Jaspers. It bears the family crest. When it spins, the hoop awakens, conjuring the corpse candles. Do you know where the talisman is?"

"The attic."

"Bring it to me. I'll keep the fire ablaze." The woman was raising her cane, trembling. "Go!"

"I'm going with you," Maisy said. Glenn gave her a look. By volunteering herself, she'd just volunteered him too. Cleek followed, and the four of them jumped on their bikes.

"Beware the bog," Lady Jasper called out, her warning echoing after them as they raced down the road. Cole sprinted ahead. He swerved into the gravel drive leading to their farmhouse. He heard crunching of gravel as the others joined him. They all dropped their bikes.

Cole led them up the creaky front porch steps and swung the screen door open. He flicked on the porch light.

The hoop was gone.

He dashed into the house and climbed the stairs. He yanked on the cord that lowered the hinged ladder, and scrambled up into the attic. Waving his arm blindly in the dark, he brushed the light bulb chain and pulled. The dim bulb only partially illuminated the room. Maisy and Cleek joined him. Glenn hesitated on the ladder.

"The hoop was over there," Cole said. He could make out an ashy crescent burned into the wall where it had rested all those years.

Maisy took a step toward him. "The whirligig?"

"Under that trunk." He tried to shove the chest, but it wouldn't budge. There was a narrow lip carved out of the bottom of the front façade, and he knew that's where the talisman had gone. On hands and knees, he tried to reach it, but the opening was too narrow.

"Here, let me," Maisy said. She crouched, resting one hand on him for support, and reached her slender arm into the darkness. Her hand slid around, searching.

"Hey, guys," Glenn said. "Did you hear something?"

They all fell silent. At first, there was nothing. Then Cole heard it. The rattle. Something rumbled across the hardwood floor downstairs, followed by the sound of shattering china.

"Holy shit, it's in the house!" Glenn yelled. He scrambled into the attic and Cole dove to haul up the ladder.

Behind him, he heard Cleek yell, "Hurry up and find it!"

"I'm trying," Maisy growled back, desperation in her voice.

Cole watched the hoop round the corner at the end of the hall below him. He slammed the trapdoor shut, panting.

"Got it!" Maisy exclaimed triumphantly. She clutched the talisman in her hand.

"Shhh..." Cole said, extending his arm.

He heard a slow *thunk thunk* as the hoop trundled across the floor beneath them. The sound gained momentum and Cole's heart went to his throat when he realized what he was hearing.

"It's rolling on the wall!" he screamed, his voice cracking.

"Help me!" he shouted to Glenn. Grunting, the two of them shoved the trunk over the trapdoor. The hoop slammed against the door so hard that the lid of the trunk popped open, then slammed down. They all backed away into the gloom, but the pounding was relentless.

"The window," Cleek said. He went to it and tried to turn the hinge. "Rusted shut," he groaned. Glenn tried it next, but no luck. Frantic, Cole ransacked the area, and grabbed a broken table leg.

"Stand back." He swung, shattering the window, sending glass flying. He yanked a canvas tarp off a chair, and tossed it across the bottom edge of the window, covering the jagged remnants of glass. Maisy handed Cole the whirligig and he stuffed it into his jeans pocket. Glenn lifted her and she shimmied through the opening, landing on the rooftop below. Cleek went next. The slamming against the trapdoor paused.

Glenn's eyes studied the hole. His voice was low when he spoke. "I don't think I can fit through there, man. You go."

Cole could see Lady Jasper's bonfire burning bright in the distance. And closer still, lights convened and bobbed over the swamp.

Glenn gave him a boost, and Cole pulled himself through the opening. He dropped down, shards of glass digging into his palms upon landing. Cleek was already cycling away, and Cole could just see Maisy's hands gripping the gutter for a moment before she dropped to the flat roof above the front porch. Cole stood and scuffed away the broken glass with his shoe. He turned back toward the window. Glenn had one arm reaching toward him, but his other shoulder was stuck. The pounding on the attic door came rapid fire, causing the entire house to quake. Cole grabbed Glenn's outstretched arm, dug his heels into the pitched rooftop, and leaned back. Glenn screamed in pain, but slipped free and dropped. Cole stumbled backward, grabbing the gutter just in time as he tumbled off the roof.

The pounding inside the house ceased.

They jumped from the porch roof and hopped on their bikes. A deafening thunder erupted from the house. Cole cut through the grass and turned just in time to see the hoop smash through the dining room window, barely missing him.

As he pedaled, Cole sensed eyes spying on him from the underbrush of the forest to the east. His heart thudded in his chest. Suddenly he heard the frantic rattle of bones as they whipped around, somersaulting faster and faster, closing in. A dark blur whirred past him, and headed straight for Maisy. Her scream cut across the field, and she veered left.

It's herding her toward the swamp.

Cole hunched forward and pumped as fast as he could. He burst ahead and smashed into the hoop. It spun into him, out of control. He heard a sick *cracking* sound above his ankle upon impact. He went soaring over the handlebars and slammed into the soggy ground.

Where did it go?

He tried to stand, but his ankle gave out, and he flopped back down, the grasses taller than his line of vision. He pushed up with his arms and caught a glimpse of his contorted bike, one rotating tire silhouetted against the sky.

The hoop crept out from behind the bike, shedding tendrils of marsh grass. It swiveled until it was pointing straight at him. Hobbled, Cole stood on one leg, searching in vain for Lady Jasper's fire. He heard Maisy calling his name, but the disorienting glow from the will-o'-the-wisps swirled around him. He'd lost all sense of direction.

He hopped blindly, when suddenly his foot began to sink. *No.* He splashed face-first into the swamp. *No no no!* Cole could hear Lady Jasper's warning in his head—*Beware the bog.* Sputtering, he hacked out a mouthful of duckweed, the musty smell of the swamp thick in his nose, bile searing the back of his throat. He was dragging himself forward by thick clumps of cattails when he felt an icy hand clamp down on his ankle. A spike of pain raced up his leg.

His scream was cut off as he was dragged under. He flailed and felt another hand grip his wrist. When he broke the surface he saw Glenn pulling him in a life-and-death tug-o-war. Cole felt a *pop* as his shoulder dislocated. Glenn was strong. The dark force controlling the hoop was stronger.

Cole used his free hand to dig in his pocket. He held the talisman out to Glenn.

"Take it to her!" he managed to choke out. Glenn hesitated,

but grabbed it, and released Cole. Gasping, Cole was dragged deeper into the bog. In his mind, he pictured Bug Jasper, his small skeletal frame perpetually at the bottom of the muck somewhere, bug-eyed mudskippers skirting in and out of his eye sockets as the hoop strolled perpetually along the bed of the swamp over the years, submerged. Admiring its handiwork. Cole didn't want to meet the same fate.

He used his good leg to kick at the hand that held him prisoner. For a moment it yielded, and he stood, waist deep in slime. Just as bony claws ripped into his shins, he saw the old woman, long gray hair billowing out in the wind, raising the talisman above her before pitching it into the fire.

The claws disappeared. Cole turned, and saw the rim of the hoop peering out above the water, like crocodile eyes. Maisy waded into the swamp, stifling her sobs, and he felt her arms embrace him. As the lights of the corpse candles grew dim and snuffed out, Wylie Bruns' hoop sank below the surface and vanished into the bog.

HEY, KAREN

Beth was standing on a stranger's driveway, holding a lopsided cranberry candle toward Carli. They were both giggling when she heard someone call her name.

"Hey, Beth!"

She turned and saw Hannah deep within the shadow of the garage, beckoning to her. Beth put the candle back among the porcelain pigs and gold-leaf candy dishes on the cluttered, dented card table. She made her way past the mid-afternoon crowd to see what Hannah wanted.

"How about these?" Hannah said, examining a teacup before setting it down. Beth's gaze drifted to the matching set. Teapot, cream and sugar, six saucers. *But only five cups.*

"Um, they're a little...floral for my taste."

"Not for you," Hannah said, her other hand draped over the handlebar of the stroller. "You mentioned you need to get Vera a birthday gift."

That was true. She'd be seeing her soon-to-be mother-in-law the following weekend, and Jay would be disappointed if she showed up with a gift card. Again.

Beth gingerly grasped a teacup, and rotated her hand. She traced the ridged scalloped edges with her fingertip. Intricate pink roses adorned the china. Reluctance dripped from her voice. "I guess these *would* match her kitchen." She haggled over the price, a part of her hoping the seller wouldn't come down. But she did. As the woman found some tissue paper and boxed up the set, she apologized for the missing cup. Said it had shattered. That her aunt must've been holding it when the stroke hit. Beth noticed the cardboard sign resting against the leg of the table, and the words written in black marker. *Estate Sale.*

Seven houses, and three purchases later, they maneuvered over a cracked sidewalk and approached Hannah's minivan. Beth waited while Hannah settled the baby in her car seat, and then collapsed the stroller. She was struggling to get it in the back, when a group of teen boys came walking down the opposite side of the street.

"So, what do you think Craig will say about the lamp?" Beth asked, still chuckling over the shark fins at the base. Hannah walked toward the driver door.

Carli laughed. "Well, I hope—"

"Hey, Karen!" one of the teens yelled, crossing the street.

Carli paused for a second, then went on. "I hope he likes it. If not, at least we can put the base of the lamp in our aquarium."

Carli set the lamp in the back of the van. Beth was still holding the box of china when one of the teens came up onto the sidewalk and approached her. His chest shoved into the back of her hands as she held the box. He got to within inches of her face.

Menacing, yet friendly, almost flirtatious, he said, *"Hey, Karen."*

One of his teeth was tipped with gold. The rest were perfect. But his breath smelled spicy. A large round stud forced his earlobe to twice its natural size. Chains shimmered across his muscled chest. Beth wasn't sure what to do to. Hannah was already in the driver's seat. *Was this a dare?* A gang dare? If she said the wrong thing, would she be stabbed? She felt herself trembling. Should she say something? The horn blared. Carli took the box from the frozen Beth, placed it in the back of the van, and slammed the hatch.

The boy broke his gaze from Beth and looked at Carli, who had folded her arms across her chest. He took a step backward, slowly nodded twice, and rejoined his friends. They giggled and continued to saunter down the street. Carli looked at Beth.

"What was that all about?"

Beth watched the gang, hoping they would continue to put distance between them and her. She relaxed her shoulders and exhaled. Her eyes lingered on the boys. "I don't know."

The next day, Beth hung the black and white print she'd found at the garage sale over the silver couch in her living room. She liked the contrast against the stark white walls. She went to the kitchen, glad she'd replaced the old appliances with stainless steel when she remodeled. Sleek, clean, pristine. She set the teakettle on to boil and made herself a cup of green tea. Watching the steam rise and swirl from a pure white mug, she felt at peace.

Beth reached for the cilantro and drank in its scent as she bagged it. She placed it in her grocery cart next to an orange bell pepper, a spaghetti squash, and a fresh loaf of focaccia bread. She finished getting the other items she needed and moved to checkout aisle number four, where she recognized her favorite cashier.

"Hi, Mrs. Patton," Beth said, placing a bottle of Merlot on the conveyor belt.

"Hey, Karen," the woman said with a smile as she retrieved the red plastic divider from the moving belt. Beth had been emptying her cart and paused, a box of fabric softener in one hand, and a bag of pretzels in the other. She felt dizzy, and gave her head a subtle shake. She put the pretzels down and brushed her straight brown bangs to the side with one finger. Then she looked at Mrs. Patton, who was scanning her items.

Blip. Blip.

"*What* did you say?"

"I said you really got a deal on those strawberries. Two packs for the price of—"

"No." She strained to keep her voice calm. "What did you *call* me?"

The cashier seemed confused for a moment. "I don't know what you—" she said, uncomfortable. *Blip.* Olive oil. *Blip.* Arugula. *Blip.*

"Beth," Beth whispered with authority, willing it to be so. She finished emptying her cart and moved up to the debit card reader. She noticed that Doug, the bag boy, had walked up. She tried to keep the tension out of her voice. Tried not to stare at the woman's nametag, resentful. *Maybe I need a nametag too.* "You always call me Beth." She swiped her card. "But just now, a moment ago, you called me Karen."

Mrs. Patton looked at her like she was crazy, then exchanged a sympathetic glance with the next woman in line. Beth focused on the numbers, punching in her code. Doug, who wore an orange and white polka dot tie, asked as he always did, if she was going to watch the game tonight.

"Do you have any coupons today, *Beth?*" the cashier asked. *Did she say it like that because I made a fuss? Or is she humoring me?*

"No." Definitely not getting a break today.

Mrs. Patton totaled her items, and gave a warm smile to the other woman in line, as though telepathing...*it'll be just a moment before I can get to you. As soon as I can get rid of this loon...*

The receipt ticked out of the register. Beth overheard the apology "about the wait" from behind her as she moved toward the exit. Doug, pushing the cart, spoke non-stop about sports as he walked her to her car. He loaded everything into her trunk. He'd always seemed a little slow, and though she'd told him every week for the past year that she wasn't into sports, he still assumed she'd be watching the big game tonight. He put the last bag in the trunk, and slammed it shut. She handed him two dollars, and walked toward the driver's door. He began wheeling her grocery cart back across the parking lot.

Feeling defeated, she said, "Have a nice day, Doug."

He turned, smiling, the sunlight shimmering off his hair. She could hear the wheels of the cart squeaking. Through his big lopsided grin, he shouted, "You too, Karen!"

She didn't feel well on Monday. Her stomach was in knots and the room spun when she tried to stand. She stumbled to the bathroom and flicked on the light. The bulb must be going bad. Her hair looked dark. Almost...black. The sight of it suddenly repulsed her. She'd worn it long, and so straight, for how many years? She grabbed a pair of scissors and began cutting until it was chin-length. After her shower, she was too exhausted to blow it dry. Seeing her reflection in her rearview mirror later, she saw natural waves she never knew she had.

Tuesday, things were slightly better. She ran into Jay in the breakroom. He smiled when he saw her enter.

"Feeling better today?"

"Uh huh." She sat down. Jay opened a cupboard behind him and pulled down two coffee mugs. He set them on the table.

"That's good. I'd hate for you to miss Mom's party this weekend." He pulled two green teabags from a cardboard box, tore open the paper, and dropped one in each mug, leaving the strings hanging loosely over the edge.

Beth didn't want to think past today, let alone about Vera's party. The image of the rose petal teacups swam through her mind. She didn't know why she'd put them in her cupboard. She'd just have to put them back in the box. *I should really get some wrapping paper.* Jay took a kettle of hot water off a burner, and poured it into each cup, steam rising.

He set the kettle back in place, and walked behind her, resting his hands on her shoulders. "I know my mom can be a bit overbearing. Some people have such strong personalities, you feel like you lose yourself in their presence." Something about the tea smelled wrong. She brought it to her lips. Green tea was her favorite, but now it seemed foul. Foreign. Jay began to massage Beth's shoulders, tender at first, but then his fingers gripped deeper into the muscle. Beth moaned. Jay lowered himself behind her, bringing his lips to her ear, whispering.

"We'll be together soon."

Then he did something he'd never done before. He ran the tip of his tongue behind her earlobe. It sent a shiver through her, but she didn't pull away. His tongue moved down her neck, flirting with the swell of her breasts. He paused then, as though bashful, even though he'd gone lower, all the way with his hands and more, several years ago and ever since. She didn't understand his hesitation. It wasn't as though they were virgins. He kissed her forehead. Then he looked into her eyes, more intently than he ever had.

"We'll be together soon, Karen."

Jay looked at his watch and winked at her before exiting the break room. She noticed he hadn't touched his tea. She left both cups cooling on the table as she went back, wobbly-kneed, to her office.

Beth sat at her kitchen table, finding the white walls, the hardwood floors, the stainless steel comforting. Carli came out of the bathroom and joined Beth. She stared into Beth's eyes.

"When did you start wearing violet contacts?"

"I didn't," Beth said, sounding defensive.

"OK. On the phone you said something weird is going on."

"Ever since the neighborhood garage sale." *Should I tell her? I've known her since seventh grade. But should I say it out loud?* "People keep calling me Karen."

Carli paused for a moment, then shoved her chair back a few inches from the table. Then she leaned forward.

"Those gang kids coming around? My cousin Scotty still has friends on the force, I could make a call—"

"No. People I *know*. The cashier at the grocery, the bag boy. My Pilates instructor. The bank teller. And a few strangers." She was so embarrassed. At how turned on she'd been by the tongue behind her ear. At how ashamed she was that her fiancé called her by another woman's name. *Say it.* "Even...Jay." *I am not going crazy. I am not crazy. I am not Karen.*

Carli's brows furrowed. "Jay?" she said, disbelieving. She ran a hand through her cropped, bleached hair. "Look, maybe the stress of work, the wedding plans, all the work you've done on this house, maybe it's just too much."

"You were *there*. You heard that kid call me Karen."

Carli nodded. "True. And I saw how much it freaked you out. You took it as some kind of threat. Maybe it traumatized you—"

"I am not imagining this."

They were both silent for a moment. Finally, Carli spoke. "I should get going. I think you need to get some rest." She walked herself to the front door, and turned back. "By the way, I love what you've done with the bathroom."

The phrase didn't even register until after the door had closed. Beth stood, and walked, then raced to the bathroom. She stood in the doorway. Where were her stark white walls? Wallpaper covered every inch. *Floral* wallpaper. She stumbled back into the entry way. The walls there were now an olive green. The hardwood floor that should've been underfoot was now a burnt-umber shag carpet.

Beth began hyperventilating. A brass sun-shaped clock she'd never seen hung near the front door, the hands spinning wildly. The doorbell rang, and she ran to it. Had Carli returned? If only she could find someone who knew her, this nightmare could end. She flung open the door and there stood…

…Danny Scheid. But, that was impossible. He'd been killed in Vietnam, hadn't he? Yet here he stood, tall as ever, a big grin on his face, and a six pack of beer in each hand, drops of water dripping from the cans onto the concrete step.

"Hey, Karen. I brought the PBR, just like you asked." He gave her a quick peck on the cheek—

On my earlobe, he was going for my earlobe…

— and moved past her into the kitchen. Right behind him was a lanky woman. Short strawberry-blond hair, bright blue eyes. The memory was swimming up to the surface…Goldie something. But hadn't she succumbed to cancer back in '73? The two chatted and made their way into the house.

Danny took in a big whiff. "Hmmm. Pot roast." He set the beer down on the Formica counter, and cracked open the oven door.

She ran over to it, scolding him, shooing him out of the kitchen. Although with his crew cut, she found it hard not to grin. "You'll let all the heat out." She closed the oven door, knowing the carrots and potatoes needed more time.

Danny was crouching near the TV now, turning the channel knob. He spoke over his shoulder.

"We're going to watch Carson tonight, right? I sure hope he does that new bit again. Did you catch it? The swami?" He chuckled to himself. "Hilarious."

Goldie went to the stove and filled the rose tea kettle with hot water. She looked so lithe, so beautiful. So alive.

"Karen," her New England accent making her a bit exotic here in the Midwest, "would you like a cup of chamomile?"

Chamomile. Of course. *That* was it. Her favorite. She opened the cupboard to the left of the sink, and pulled down two teacups and saucers. She remembered how much she loved bridge night. The comforting smell of dinner. The familiar sound of her friends' chatter. The warmth of the chamomile tea as she sipped it from her favorite rose petal teacups.

Someone came scrambling up the front porch steps. Danny headed for the door as he said, "I hope it's OK, I invited a friend." A moment later he and another man walked into the kitchen.

"There's someone I'd like you to meet," Danny said. They joined the other guests enjoying the pot roast around the table. "This is Bert."

The young man held out his hand. "It's a real pleasure."

She set down a tray of warm cinnamon rolls, took off her oven mitts, and wiped her hands on her cross-stitched apron.

"Call me Karen," she said, smiling from ear to ear, thinking how good it felt to be home.

A USED INFINITY

"Left turn up ahead in one quarter mile."
"I know," Vinnie said. He'd gotten off the highway on impulse, and she wasn't having it. Her voice was starting to grate on his nerves already. Not that there was anything wrong with her voice. The voice itself was pleasant. Sexy even. It was how she was always correct that bothered him. How she wanted to be in charge, and seemed calmly annoyed when he didn't follow her directions exactly. Just for the heck of it, he ignored the turn and kept going.

"Make a legal U-turn at the earliest opportunity." The sound was sultry, but subtly bossy.

"I'm taking a detour. Getting some coffee." He didn't bother asking her if she wanted one. He turned onto the apparent main drag and searched for a Starbucks. He spotted one, but then he pictured himself trying to juggle the coffee, the gear shift and all the other gadgets on the dash. The image didn't end well. He thought better of drinking in the car. He didn't want to chance spilling anything on the leather seats. He'd only had this ride for less than an hour, and wanted to keep her pristine.

Vinnie pulled back out into traffic, then realized he'd gotten turned around. Wasn't sure which way was home. She didn't disappoint.

"Please proceed to the highlighted route."

His buddy at the auction house on the outskirts of Chicago had raved about the GPS system. *Once you get used to this baby, it'd be a heartache to give her up.* The handbook for the GPS was more detailed than the one for the car. Vinnie figured he'd read it when he got back to Louisville. For now, he didn't know how to turn the damn thing off. But since he was lost, maybe that was just as well. And he figured he could put up with her for another few hours. Especially since she'd have nothing to say so long as he stayed on the highway.

It was Friday afternoon. He drove with his left hand firmly at ten o'clock on the wheel, and his right palm poised over the horn, ready to honk at anyone who got too close. He thought about the look on Pam's face when she'd see this car for the first time. She may've gotten the house and the kids, but he got enough to buy a new car. Well, all right, a used car, but it might as well be new. And he'd quit his job two days ago. He was thirty-nine, and the marriage had been officially dissolved last week. He thought *dissolved* seemed like a funny word for it, but appropriate. He'd sworn to Pam his life would be better now. He almost threatened to move home to Chicago, but he couldn't leave the kids. So he'd gotten an apartment, was getting the car, would look for a better job. *You better start practicing*, she'd sneered. *Would you like paper or plastic?* Then she'd laughed, that annoying cat-with-its-tail-caught-in-a-blender laugh of hers that her new boyfriend was now stuck with. Yeah, Vinnie Zaborak was certain that it was time for some major changes. He'd pull up for an interview in this black luxury vehicle that screamed success, and he was sure he could land any job he wanted.

Those thoughts stayed on his mind as he drove south on I-65. A half hour later, the GPS spoke up.

"Please check fuel gauge."

I thought these things just gave directions. He glanced at the fuel level. Two-thirds full. He kept driving. A couple minutes later, he heard her again.

"Please check fuel gauge." Her voice was so polite, but determined. It reminded him of those girls in college. Women hadn't changed all that much in twenty years. The hot ones knew they were hot. It never mattered what they were saying, it was how they were saying it. *Get me a drink. Let me copy your homework.* He always gave in. Today he had plenty of gas, but she began to repeat her instruction. Sexy or not, now she was getting on his nerves. He pulled off at the next exit, and filled up the tank. That quieted her for another hundred miles.

"Please check fuel gauge. Exit to the right in one half mile." He'd seen the sign for the exit to Seymour, Indiana.

"What are you talking about? We're heading back to Louisville."

"Exit to the right in one quarter mile."

Vinnie touched the GPS screen with his right index finger, hoping to find an off button. Instead it pulled up a menu of previously loaded destinations. It made him feel like a peeping Tom, like he was spying on someone else's history. The one that was highlighted didn't have a street address. Just said "avoid area." And it looked like it was in BFE. Some moron at the auction must've forgotten to clear them. Most of the locations were in or around Seymour. Maybe she had a screw loose and was guiding him to one of these. He decided he wanted that cup of coffee after all. Would take a break inside a coffee shop, and read over the manual for a few minutes.

He took the exit.

He couldn't find a familiar coffee chain, but settled for a diner. Vinnie took a sip of his coffee, burned his tongue, and set the cup down. Ten minutes of sifting through the GPS handbook didn't help. He pulled out his cell phone, something he *had* learned to program, and called his buddy at the auction.

"Chi-Town's Bump & Trade." Hers was definitely not a sexy voice. Not the kind of girl who was used to getting what she wanted. More like the kind of girl who was used to rolling out of bed, hacking out what was left in her lungs from the previous night's cigarettes, to greet another who's-going-to-annoy-me-today kind of day.

"This is Vinnie Zaborak." Emphasis on the *bore*, he thought. Old habits die hard. Not so boring anymore, he reminded himself. "Got a question for Scotty about a car I drove off the lot this morning."

No transition, just a click, and a computerized guy's voice informing him that he was now enjoying the sound of the Chicago Symphony Orchestra. Seemed a bit presumptive, even for a computer voice, to tell him whether or not he was enjoying it.

"Vinnie? How's she treating you?" Scotty said.

"All right so far," Vinnie said. "The GPS though, it's kinda freakin' me out. Ditched my ex to get rid of that kind of side-seat driver. I think it's got a glitch. Telling me to check the gas when I've got practically a full tank. And she's trying to direct me to places in Seymour. Tell me you didn't sell me a lemon."

"Get the wax outta yo' ears, Vinnie. GPS don't give low tank warnings. So far as a lemon, make lemonade. Hang on a minute, let me check her birth record." Once again, he was informed that he was enjoying the symphony orchestra.

"Vinnie?" Scotty's South-side accent was a pitch higher. "There is somethin' a little off here. Looks like she needed some work done when she came in. New grill, new windshield. Says the guy hit a deer. But the grease monkeys signed off on her. Said she's good as new."

So much for full disclosure.

"You got the guy's name? The one who hit the deer? Maybe he can tell me how to de-program her until I get up to speed."

"Vinnie, you know I'm not supposed to—"

"—Sell lemons to second cousins or loyal customers, with lots of potential referrals."

He moaned but consented, and gave Vinnie the name and number of the previous owner. Vinnie got back in the car and turned the engine on. He dialed the number.

"Bradley Torrence," a voice said. Scotty had told him the name was Brad Torrence. The guy answering the phone, calling himself *Bradley* made Vinnie wonder if this was a mistake. *Bradley* was the name for a guy who bought new cars. Probably traded the car for a Beemer. And probably wouldn't want to be bothered by a guy whose name had the emphasis on *bore*. A guy who bought someone else's leftovers.

"Hey, Bradley." He almost choked on the name, and was suddenly self-conscious of his own South-side accent. "My name's Vinnie Zaborak." *Damn, I should have said Vincent.* "I know this is going to sound a little weird, but I just bought a car at auction this morning." He decided to lie to keep Scotty out of trouble. "I found your name and number on the bill of sale in the glove box."

"Yes," he said, annoyance creeping through the phone line. "What about it?"

"It's the GPS." *She*, he was tempted to say. "It keeps trying to direct me to an 'avoid area' on your old program. Some place near the quarries."

For a minute he wondered if the guy had hung up. Finally, Bradley spoke. "That damn thing never did work right. But I washed my hands of it. She's your problem now." There was a loud click and the line went dead. Not exactly the Hoosier hospitality he'd been hoping for.

He was idling in the diner parking lot. He caught his reflection in the rearview mirror. *What am I doing?* Pushing forty, as Pam had told him for the last five years. Why was he so anxious to get back to Louisville? He wouldn't see the kids until the following weekend. He didn't even have a pet at home waiting for him. Why had he quit his job on the spur of the moment with a backup plan no grander than to drive up in a good-looking car? *Stupid stupid stupid.* His throat felt tight, the way it had six months ago when Pam had said she was seeing someone. "Like a shrink?" he'd asked. "No, Vinnie," she'd said. The look on her face said, *no, Vinnie, you dumbass.* He tilted the mirror away, like he was embarrassed for the car to see him cry. He looked at the navigation screen.

She was directing him to a new location about a mile away. One that hadn't even been on the list of previous destinations. What the hell. It was almost rush hour. Better to putz around here for a bit, let traffic die down a little. Besides, Vinnie decided if he went to the highlighted location, maybe that would appease her and he could finish the rest of the drive in peace.

He pulled up in front of a bungalow.

"You have reached your destination," she said.

Sitting there, he wondered how he would get back to I-65 if the GPS started spouting off other addresses. He decided it might not hurt for once to ask for directions. He got out of the car, and used the remote to lock it. The walkway to the front door of the bungalow consisted of concrete slabs, most of them cracked or crumbling. Vinnie spied his morphed reflection in a shiny green metallic ball nestled on a concrete stand in the garden. He walked to the front door and rang the doorbell.

He heard heavy footsteps approaching from inside, and a

guy opened the door. He was tall, and looked to be in his mid-twenties. He didn't say anything but looked disappointed when he saw Vinnie. Like he'd been expecting someone else.

"Sorry to bother you," Vinnie said, "but I'm trying to get back to the highway, and I seem to have gotten a bit turned around."

The guy's shoulders relaxed. "Come on in," he said, taking a step back.

Vinnie stepped inside and found himself in a small living room with hardwood floors. From the floral pattern on the sofa, he guessed the guy lived here with a wife, thinking of the curtains Pam had made him suffer with for twenty years. For some reason Vinnie had a fleeting thought that if this had been the eighties, the guy would have had a mullet. As it was, his hair was close cropped.

"I got a map around here somewhere." He started rummaging through drawers. "Now, where did she put those?" he said under his breath. Vinnie noticed framed photographs lining the hall that led to the kitchen. He took a closer look and congratulated himself for his keen eye. Mr. Woulda-had-a-mullet was in the photos, with a very attractive brunette. One photo was just the girl. She had short curly hair. The background was blurry, some kind of carnival. Only the girl was in focus. She wore a red knee-length dress and a small red hat. She wasn't looking directly at the camera. Not out of shyness, just not caring who was looking at her. The camera had caught her in mid-laugh, an expression that seemed like it belonged there on her face. He wondered what her laugh sounded like.

Just then their answering machine went off. Vinnie heard a woman's voice.

"Hi, it's Gabby." Then she said what number the caller had reached. "Digger and I are home, but we have better things to do than talk to you," and suddenly Vinnie knew exactly what her laughter sounded like. He imagined the shoulda-had-a-mullet guy kissing the back of her neck as she recorded the message. Only something intimate can send off that particular kind of laughter. "We'll call you back with a blow-by-blow on what our ceiling looks like. Leave a message."

It was the *leave a message* that did it. Still sultry, but a little bossy. Vinnie spun in a slow, hesitant arc, and looked out the window to his Infiniti, sitting curbside. Resting. He felt a ringing in his ears like he was going to faint and realized he'd stopped breathing. The voice that had been annoying him, bossing him, directing him. Haunting him all day. It was the same as the voice on the machine.

He looked more closely at the photos on the wall. Gabby and Digger sitting on a haystack in the bed of his pickup. What he presumed to be Gabby's and Digger's feet dangling over the end of a dock, sun rippling off the lake, their faces just murky reflections in the water below. The carnival photo. The one he now thought of as 'Gabby in Red Dress.' He studied it.

She wore a small red knit hat. The red sundress. A silver oval locket on a braided chain around her neck. Not quite looking at the camera. Very little makeup, none that he could detect other than her lipstick.

He jumped when he heard her voice again. "Hi, it's Gabby." Vinnie turned and saw that Digger had hit the play button. No one had left a message, but Digger seemed drawn to that voice. "…we have better things to do than talk to you…"

"Your girlfriend?" Vinnie asked, trying very hard to sound natural. Now being thankful for his accent, hoping his Italian charm could mask the nervous breakdown he suspected he was having.

"Yeah," Digger said. Distracted. Then more focused, apologetic. "I don't know where she put the maps. Lord knows they weren't in her car."

"Excuse me?"

"Gabby," Digger said, gesturing toward the photos. "She never was good with directions. About a month ago, we had a fight about getting married. Me wanting to, her telling me for the zillionth time 'no.' Took off in her car. They found it later, near the quarries. Gas tank was empty, so the sheriff figured she'd got lost, run out of gas, and started walking. Either kept on walking or—"

Met with foul play. Digger didn't seem to be able to say it out loud, but Vinnie knew that's what he was thinking.

"The first week or so, I kept trying to convince myself she never really woulda left me. The more days go by, the more I'm hoping she did. Considering the alternative. Don't want to believe either one. Guess I'm trying to pick the lesser evil of the two, you know what I mean?"

Considering he'd just realized either his car was possessed by the spirit of a missing girl, or he was losing his mind, Vinnie knew exactly what he meant. Only he hadn't had a month to think it over, and hadn't decided yet which one was worse.

They stood there for a minute, Vinnie wanting to get out of this house, but dreading getting back in his car. He figured Digger was probably wondering why he was telling all this to a stranger. But who knows, maybe when you're going through something like that, you'll tell anyone who'll listen. Digger broke the silence.

"Just turn your car around, go left at the second light. You'll see the signs for the highway."

Vinnie walked slowly down the crumbling walk. He used the remote to unlock the car. It beeped at him, and flashed the parking lights. Like it was saying hello.

He moved gingerly into the seat, wondering, is she everywhere? Is she just the GPS? Or the whole car? He turned the fob and waited. He could almost hear her breathing.

"Where to now?" Nothing. Like she didn't want to leave the house. Didn't want to leave Digger.

"Gabby? Where to?"

The engine sputtered, like she was clearing her throat. "Please proceed to the highlighted route." He tried to tell himself it was just his imagination, but she sounded sad. The highlighted route ended at the avoid area.

Vinnie knew he could've taken Digger's directions and found the highway. And if he was still the guy with the emphasis on *bore*, that's exactly what he would have done. But he needed to find out what was happening. Besides, if he took his way instead of hers, he'd just have to listen to her commanding him to turn around. And they both knew he'd give in.

He looked at the "avoid area," on the screen. As he pulled away from the curb he realized with some trepidation that the sun was setting behind him. After they'd gotten out of town, she spoke softly.

"Turn up the heat." Her voice sounded so synthesized.

"It's fine, it's already at seventy-four."

"I'm cold, Vincent. Please turn up the heat." Suddenly he was cold too, and he punched the red arrow repeatedly until the interior heat registered eighty-six degrees. His teeth were chattering. He turned the blower up higher. He had to be hallucinating. The stress of the divorce. The mid-life crisis. For Christ sakes, she'd said his frigging name.

"Do you want any music?" he asked, his voice cracking.

"Caution. Slow down."

They were on a back road. A cornfield to one side, woods to the other. Vinnie saw no other traffic. He kept going.

"Vincent, stop!" she commanded. Her voice no longer sounded so computerized. He slammed on the brakes, and a dog darted out in front of him. It was mangy and whimpering. Vinnie was shaking.

"Proceed to the highlighted route."

Vinnie started up again, slowly.

"Caution. Approaching merge point."

He didn't see where any traffic could be merging. It was a two-lane back road. He came over a hill, the kind kids would call a roller coaster.

His headlights caught a girl as he crested the rise. Her chocolate-brown eyes grew large and the impact flung her up on to the hood of his car. But she didn't stop. Her head crashed through the windshield. Vinnie felt the seatbelt catch him. The girl lay with her legs on the hood, her head and torso protruding into the car. She was a mangled mess. A thick trail of blood ran down in a dark rivulet from her scalp. She tried to speak, but her jaw looked dislocated, and nothing came out but a garbled moan. She reached for him.

Shaking, Vinnie moved to hold her hand, and she vanished.

The car sat, idling on the lonely country road. The windshield was solid. Vinnie unbuckled, and swung open his door, getting out. The door still ajar, the car engine purring, he heard the wind rustle the adjacent cornfield. He screamed into the night and dropped to his knees on the pavement. He was losing his mind. He suddenly felt an overwhelming sense of empathy for Digger. Sometimes two possibilities were heartbreaking. But one was inevitably more devastating.

Vinnie stood, his "pushing-forty" knees complaining. He looked both ways, and thought he saw the mongrel he'd almost hit slinking off down the road. The corn stalks rippled, whispered, and he shivered. He approached the car and stood between the open door and the driver's seat. He leaned his head in.

"Please proceed to the highlighted route."

On the screen was a computerized image of his car. Vinnie shuddered when he saw the section that was highlighted. The trunk.

He considered leaving the car. Just walking away. But then that would be giving in. Accepting that he was losing his mind.

He popped the trunk and readied himself for the sight of the decomposing body of Gabby, the girl who had once worn a red dress and studied her bedroom ceiling. Instead he saw nothing. Just an empty trunk. He was about to close it when something shimmered in the moonlight. He reached in and pulled the thing out. A braided silver chain, with an oval locket. Hand trembling, he took it and got back in the driver's seat.

Engraved on the locket was a scripted letter "G." Vinnie opened the locket, feeling like he was reading someone's diary. It was a photo of an old woman, her hair pulled back in a loose bun, cheek to cheek with a girl of about ten. Mirror images, matching dimples and smiling eyes. Without thinking, Vinnie hung the chain over the rearview mirror. He shut the engine off.

"OK, Gabby. I know how you died. You want Digger to know, right? That you didn't leave him by choice? That's what this is all about?" *How do I tell him? I saw a vision? I found the locket?*

"Vincent, it's time to go."

"I'm not sure I can go anywhere with you," he said. He tried to put his hands at ten o'clock and two o'clock on the wheel, but they were trembling. "I'm kind of freaking out."

"Vincent, a danger zone is approaching. It's time to go."

Vinnie turned the fob and the engine roared into life. He saw headlights approaching. An SUV slowed down and the other driver rolled down his window.

"Everything OK, buddy?" the guy asked.

A dead girl's ghost has just splattered in my lap. Everything was definitely not OK.

"I got a little turned around. Mind if I follow you out of here?"

"No problem. The back way's the quickest."

Vinnie followed as the guy led him off the paved road into a clearing between the trees. Vinnie stayed on his tail lights.

The guy led him farther back into the woods on a logging road. The Infiniti bumped and splashed. The GPS screen showed fewer and fewer real roads, and more and more blue blotches.

The quarries.

"Vincent, turn around," Gabby said.

"You aren't real. You're in my mind, and once I get out of here, I'm having you turned off, permanently." Surely there must be happy pills that make talking GPS systems go away.

The car ahead of his slowed down. Vinnie stopped, and put the car in park. He got out of the car. The other guy was looking behind him. The guy's cell phone rang. "Bradley Torrence," he said. Now what are the odds of that? He told the caller he'd get back to them. Vinnie realized he'd just reached the danger zone. He started stammering.

"I-I-I think I can find my way from here, th-thanks."

"Not so fast," Bradley said. "I came out here to make sure her body's still here. After I got your call, I started wondering if she somehow survived. Are you screwing with me? There's no way. She was dead when she went in the water."

They both turned when the voice spoke from the interior of Vinnie's car.

"Vincent, get in the car."

"Who is that?" demanded Bradley, paranoia evident in his voice. "What is this? Blackmail for the hit and run? I made her disappear once, I can do it again." He moved, but Vinnie moved faster. He dove into the car and slammed the door. Bradley was reaching into his own car for something.

"Go around him, then follow the path to the right," Gabby said. Her command was punctuated by gunshots coming from Bradley.

Vinnie did as he was told. He sped past Bradley, his spinning tires sending forest floor and muck all over Bradley's clothes. He fishtailed as he took the right turn. His pursuer had jumped into his own car and was following him.

Tree branches whipped the windshield in rapid succession, *thunk thunk thunk.*

"Faster," Gabby said.

"I can't see where I'm going!" Vinnie yelled.

"Curve to the left, one-sixteenth of a mile," Gabby said.

"What?" And then he saw it, the brief warning helping. He gripped the wheel tighter and moved into the turn. Behind him, Bradley hadn't been prepared and his SUV sideswiped a tree, hanging him up for a few precious seconds.

He glanced at the GPS screen, the only way he knew how to make eye contact with Gabby. The grayed-out avoid area was rapidly approaching, and with a sickening sense Vinnie realized the outline was the shape of a woman. It could be any woman, wearing a knit cap perhaps, and a knee-length dress. But he knew it was Gabby.

"We're almost there Vincent." He started to panic, thinking maybe she wanted a partner in her cold watery grave, and that she was leading him to that end. Then the back windshield exploded and a bullet whizzed past the rearview mirror. The silver chain jounced.

The surface under the tires was changing from dirt and gravel-covered road to wooden planks. The car rumbled uphill, his headlights revealing nothing, like being on a roller coaster and not being able to see the drop. As he crested the hill he heard her final command.

"Hard right, Vincent. *Now.*"

He closed his eyes for a moment, and cranked the wheel to the right. The SUV was right behind. Vinnie plowed through a row of bushes, and the car came to rest on a fallen log. He jumped out and ran back to see Bradley's vehicle. He hadn't taken the hard right, and had followed the boat ramp straight into the lake. Vinnie saw shadowy fervent movement inside the car as it sank. His adrenaline pumping, he ran back to his Infiniti, wishing he could hug Gabby. Or at least give her a high-five.

"Gabby, we did it! We did it! We're alive." He was so relieved not to have died, it took him a moment to absorb the consequences of what had just happened. Gabby was silent.

He called 911. Said that when he and Bradley had spoken earlier, Bradley asked him to meet out here. Phone records would confirm the call. Once he got here, Bradley admitted he'd run her over by accident, but put her in the trunk, and disposed of her body in the quarry.

One of the first officers on the scene said due to the cold temperature of the water, she should be almost perfectly preserved.

He watched as a sheriff's car pulled up, and Digger jumped out. In the glare of the headlights, Vinnie could see he'd been crying. The dive team came to search for her. Another team hauled the SUV out, a lifeless Bradley still inside. Vinnie didn't go near when they pulled Gabby from the lake. She wasn't there. Not really. She hadn't been there for quite some time. Not since the merge point. He felt a tinge of guilt.

The wrecker helped pull his car off the log, and aside from a few scratches and the shattered rear window, it seemed ok. They asked if he had insurance. Of course he did.

He slid into the seat, leaving the window down in spite of the cold night air.

"OK, Gabby, let's go home."

The car remained silent, and he tried to tell himself she just needed some time. They'd been through a lot today. He touched the GPS screen and a woman's voice said, "Please proceed to the highlighted route." But the voice wasn't sultry. It wasn't sexy.

It wasn't Gabby.

Just the synthesized voice of a woman who'd been paid to give directions to guys who seemed to always be lost.

He called Digger's number, waiting for her voice to pick up. He would record the message onto his phone and listen to her laughter. He stroked the silver locket, knowing that Gabby had moved on to her final merge point. That she was on her way to using her infinity. Scotty was right. She was going to be a heartache to give up. But Vinnie was comforted knowing she was no longer cold or lost or alone.

He put the car in gear, and drove into the darkness, one hand relaxed on the wheel. And he promised himself he'd never let the gas run lower than half a tank. Out of respect to a girl who'd only wanted to find her way safely home.

A BONE TO PICK

Even before that chunk of limestone found its way into her skull, most folks in Posey County had an opinion about Molene Mueller. Those who felt sorry for her after the accident lied, and said she'd always been a sweet child. Thoughtful. An angel. Then there were those who admitted that she'd been odd. Teched in the head. Most folks also had an opinion about how that rock came to find itself embedded in her forehead. The girl didn't remember the day of the accident. Some hailed Thad Lyre a hero for pulling her out of the Wabash. The river was raging that day, and he'd risked a drowning. A few others, especially after a night at the tavern, were pretty convinced it was Thad who'd helped her into the river, and that he and that rock had conspired to leave her there.

Even at the age of seven, Molene was a tall girl. Lanky, almost skeletal. Her dark hair hung limp, her ears sticking out. The middle child in a German family of seven, she spent most of her afternoons on the banks of the Wabash fishing with her brother, Kaspar, while her dad worked at the mill and their mother tended the home.

Kaspar would sneak bits of chicken liver onto his hook to lure in the channel catfish their father loved to eat. Molene would slide her hook through a live minnow, careful not to tear the thing apart, and then watched her bobber drift on the surface of the water. She and Mamzy favored the sweet filets of the black crappie that were spawning.

One morning Kaspar sent Molene to dig for night crawlers. Their cousins were coming for dinner, and he wanted to catch enough bass to feed the brood. Molene went to her room to slip out of her nightshirt into a jumper. She heard a thud as something slammed into the warped glass of her window. She slipped outside, the dew cool against her pale bare feet.

She took a stick and began to stir the dirt in Mamzy's flower bed. It didn't take long before she spied what she was after. Thick and red, pulsating and slimy, the night crawlers tried to squirm away. Molene tossed the stick away, and let her fingers move through the flower bed. She felt something warm, even though nothing warm belonged here.

The delicate bird fit perfectly in her delicate hand. Its neck was broken, the head drooping in a way that would have made her sisters cry. She looked up at the window and saw a slight smudge. The bird had left something of itself on the glass. Molene wondered if any part of it might be useful in catching tonight's feast, pondering what the bass would prefer. She tucked the bird under the hydrangeas. After filling her cup with more worms, she ran to the river bank to join her brother.

A few days later, Molene awoke to the sound of raindrops pelting her window. She lay still, her little sister's feet pressed against her back, and studied the way the raindrops swerved around the smudge left by the bird. She waited until she heard Mamzy in the kitchen, putting on a kettle of coffee, and then she slunk out through her window.

Her feet sank into the earth, and the scent was one of her favorites. That after-rain smell. But something else tried to sneak in there. Something rotten. Something dead. Molene felt around under the hydrangeas and found the little bird. Mamzy could name every bird in Posey County just by listening to its song, or seeing it flit by. Molene wished she'd paid attention. It seemed like the thing might have been a chickadee, but she couldn't be sure. It really wasn't a bird anymore. Just a carcass. Some of its feathers were still intact, but one side looked like an open wound. Little dark organs hid behind delicate white bones. Maggots squirmed inside, and even as Molene held the thing, flies buzzed and tried to alight upon it. She began scooping moist earth to make a shallow grave with one hand. She'd really only meant to bury it. But as she moved to place the chickadee in its shallow grave, her fingers touched the bones.

She had a vision. She was soaring over the Wabash. When she yanked her hand away from the carcass, the vision was gone. Molene heard her little sister's cry through the window. She was either having a nightmare, or had just awoken from one. Molene reached out and touched the little bird's bones again.

She saw things even the bird would not have remembered. The darkness and the pecking, struggling to break free of the egg shell. Stretching her neck hoping for one giant gulp of whatever her mother regurgitated, her siblings stretching and crying beside her in the nest. Stumbling from the edge and falling to the ground for the first time. Every day a struggle, searching for food, for water, for shelter.

Molene moved her hands along the fine bones and saw herself evading predators. She saw herself as Molene through the window. Saw herself as the bird striking the window and felt her neck snap. She felt the last few desperate pumps of blood in her veins as her eyes glazed over beneath the hydrangeas.

Her mother was calling to her now, alerted to her absence by her younger sister's cries. But Molene kept stroking the bones. She felt the tickle of the flies as they landed on her feathers. The first movement of the maggots as they fed on her flesh.

She heard her mother's heavy footfalls moving toward the door. Molene shoved the dead bird deep into her pocket with one hand as she plucked a blue bloom, still wet from the morning rain, in the other. She'd never been good at smiling, but as the door swung open and the smell of grilling sausages hit her, Molene held the flower out as an offering. One hand still deep in her pocket, she watched her bird-self kill and swallow a wasp. Mamzy's face softened when she saw the flower, and she told Molene to wash up for breakfast.

When Kaspar went to Korea, the whole house became more sullen than usual. Father worked longer hours. Mamzy took on more seamstress jobs from the town ladies, hand sewing beads and pearls and sequins onto the dresses their daughters would wear to spring formals. Mamzy never even seemed to notice when she pricked her finger until the little ones would point out the dots of blood on the gowns. Then the house would smell like vinegar as she worked to rub out the stains.

Molene watched how her family struggled. Father with his work. Mamzy with trying to be accepted by the town ladies and worrying over her oldest son. Molene had turned eight over the summer but she knew what war was. She'd seen it on the television at Mr. Summers' hardware store. As she sorted Mamzy's beads and pearls, Molene wondered about Kaspar's struggles. Before that morning in the rain, she'd never given a thought to the struggles of a bird. Now she wondered about the plight of every creature around her.

Once school started up again, sometimes the other children saw her with her little box. Her pet. She tried to hide it, to be subtle, but seven hours was too long to go without taking flight. The day after Sandy Tyson's dog got hit by the milk truck, Molene approached her near the monkey bars, and offered to bury it. The girl saw it as a kindness, and they walked to Sandy's house after school. Molene was tender. She and Sandy dug the hole together. Molene suggested that Sandy get something special to put in the grave. Something that meant a lot to the dog. When the girl disappeared into the house, the porch door slamming shut, Molene used Kaspar's fishing knife to open the dog's belly. She felt around for a rib and snapped it off. Even in the few seconds that she held the bone before dropping it into her pocket, she sensed how much that dog loved its human family. Molene rolled the dog over so the wound wouldn't show. Sandy came rushing back with a well-gnawed T-bone. Tears ran down her cheeks as she placed it in the grave. The girls worked together to cover the dog with loose dirt. For close to an hour, Molene sat stoic, listening while Sandy told stories about her dog. And all the while, Molene stroked the bone. She saw her puppy-self pushing past a dead sibling to make its way to the light, its mother licking the birth sac away. Nursing. Hunting. She spent weeks with the bone, learning how to read it. How to focus, how to find unearthed memories. She felt a sharp pain along the scar in her forehead when she was jolted by the vision of Thad Lyre kicking the dog.

A Bone to Pick

It was October when they got word that Kaspar had died. The army sent his body back in a box. The night before the burial, Molene snuck into the mortuary. She had to see him again, but when she lifted the lid of the casket she realized they had lied to her.

Her brother's body wasn't there. The mortician admitted the beautiful casket was ornamental for the boys who didn't come back whole. The box he'd be buried in was in the back room. Molene didn't cry. She didn't ask permission. When the mortician left the room to answer the bell, she walked back there. She lifted the lid of the plain pine box and looked at the parts. A leg blown off just above the knee was still in a boot. She saw a helmet, lifted it, and on closer inspection realized that a clod of hair and a fragment of skull had become fused to the helmet. Some body parts were unrecognizable. Molene went to work.

The foot belonged to another boy who had grown up in the South. Molene watched her Southern boy-self square dance and eat Georgia peaches, juice dribbling down his chin. She touched other remnants and shuddered at the images of war. She lifted the helmet, allowing her fingertips to brush the bone fragments. She saw the familiar dirt floor of their home. She rode across the Wabash on a flat boat headed to the Ohio to unload a freighter. She felt her Kaspar-self tackling Thad Lyre, punching his face, and asking what had happened to his sister. He and Thad had been vying for the same girl, and only a week before, Thad threatened that he'd be sorry if he didn't back down. That if Kaspar took the one he loved most, Thad would do the same. As Kaspar threw another punch, he wondered if Molene was paying the price for his challenging a Lyre. That day on the river bank, Thad denied it. Kaspar didn't have proof, but he didn't believe him either. He cradled Molene as the blood ran down her face, and through Kaspar, she saw herself lifeless.

Molene took the helmet and ignored the mortician's weak protests as she walked out the door. She never fell asleep that night. Instead, she caressed the bone, and saw the ceiling her brother was looking at. A thatched roof and a gray sky. Her head was throbbing, a chunk of the skull missing. At the graveside the next morning, she told her mother that Kaspar wasn't really dead.

It seemed a comfort to Mamzy, who choked back tears. "That's right my love. None of us ever are."

After the pine box was lowered, and the family mourned, Molene awaited her brother's return.

Mamzy thought Molene went to the cemetery to pay her respects to Kaspar. But Kaspar wasn't there. She went to the cemetery and thought of all the bones. All the memories. All the secrets. The great families who had ruled Posey County. Freya Lyre, Devoted Mother. No mention of what kind of wife she'd been. A tree that had been struck by lightning stood over the Lyre crypt. She wished trees had bones. She would like to know that tree's story, to see what it had seen. There was no way to dig up any of the bones all around, but Molene would lie on the ground, her long slender fingers sweeping through the grass, and imagine she could hear them breathing. She strained to hear their whispers.

The night before Thanksgiving, Molene sat under the tree in the cemetery, stroking her brother's skull bone. His pain had subsided. He couldn't feel his legs anymore. A woman with a kind face tried to get him to drink water, but he could no longer swallow. Molene saw through his eyes as the thatched roof faded to darkness. She felt the woman place a thin sheet over his body and say soft words in a language she couldn't understand.

The next morning as the scent of roast turkey and red cabbage spread through house, Molene did something she'd never done. She cried. When her father asked who wanted to break the wishbone, Molene deferred to her younger siblings. She began crying again and Mamzy asked her to help clear the dishes. Once they were alone in the kitchen, her mother lifted Molene's face gently by the chin. She didn't speak, but her raised brows were asking what was wrong.

"Kaspar is dead."

Mamzy looked deep into her eyes. They were almost the same height. Her voice was soft when she spoke. "I know little one, I know."

That night, after Father had smoked his pipe and everyone

had gone to bed, Molene took a looking glass and snuck down to the river bank. She studied her scar in the mirror. She pressed her fingertip into her scar, but flesh and blood blocked her view of how it got there. She took Kaspar's knife from her pocket. She'd seen him gut and filet fish hundreds of times. The blade was sharp. Molene pulled out a box of matches and struck one. She let the flame lick the blade. She rested the mirror in the crook of a tree, and made a small slice in her forehead, right along the edge of her scar. She needed to know how she got this gift. This curse. She needed to know Thad Lyre's role in it. As a trickle of blood flowed toward her brow, Molene wondered which of Thad's bones she would study if it turned out he'd been her attacker rather than her savior.

As the moon rose high, Molene peeled back a flap of flesh, and pressed her finger to the bone.

ABOUT THE AUTHOR

Marianne Halbert is an author from central Indiana. She loves creepy, atmospheric, unsettling horror. Her biggest inspirations are Shirley Jackson, Rod Serling, Daphne du Maurier, and Ray Bradbury. Much of her work has been described as "literary horror" or "quiet horror". Marianne creates imperfect characters who break your heart and make you think of them long after the page has closed. Her stories have appeared in *ThugLit, Necrotic Tissue Magazine,* and numerous other magazines and anthologies on the cutting edge of dark speculative fiction. Marianne has been on panels at AnthoCon and Necon, is a member of the Horror Writers Association and a member of Sisters in Crime. She's also a lawyer, mental health advocate, wife, mother of two young adult daughters, and wrangler of her family's mini-goldendoodle, Ripley. Marianne has two collections out, *Wake Up and Smell the Creepy* and *Cold Comforts*. She is currently working on her first novel, *The Lady's Pocket*. Keep up with her at:

https://www.halbertfiction.com
@HalbertFiction on Twitter
@HalbertFiction on Facebook

Wake up and smell the creepy!

Curious about other Crossroad Press books?
Stop by our site:
http://store.crossroadpress.com
We offer quality writing
in digital, audio, and print formats.

Made in the USA
Columbia, SC
01 December 2020